Brendan Sean Sullivan

Irish Blood

Copyright © 2013 by Brendan Sean Sullivan

All Rights Reserved. No part of this book may be reproduced, scanned, or distributed in printed or electronic form without permission.

This book is a work of fiction. Names, characters and events are a product of the author's imagination and any resemblance to any person, living or dead, is coincidental.

Irish Blood

To my Annie.

Chapter 1

THE CHURCH WAS COLD. As Mick tasted the salty water leaking from his right eye onto his lips, the cathedral organ droned the Peace Prayer of St. Francis. He had heard the song many times before, but now its words were so intense. Never did he imagine he would hear them at the funeral of his dead wife. Even the words "dead wife" echoed in his head like something unreal.

The last week was a complete blur. He could barely recall the details of the events that had brought him back to the United States. Sarah's body being loaded into the black coroner's van, the required body identification at the Belfast City Morgue, the half-assed murder investigation, the unloading of her coffin on the tarmac back at JFK airport in New York City, the funeral arrangements which he had insisted on handling – how did it all happen?

Mick's father whispered, "It's time son," and helped him to his feet as Sarah's coffin was wheeled down the center aisle and loaded into the hearse waiting outside the doors of Saint Matthew's Church where they were married. The three mile limousine ride to the McKenna family plot seemed to take forever. The long train of vehicles twisted and turned like a snake, winding through the all too small cemetery roads for what seemed like an eternity, then, finally stopped. Mick gathered his strength and stepped out into the uncharacteristically frigid March air. The sun cut through the thick cirrus clouds with blinding intensity. As Mick and Sarah's brothers carried the coffin to its final resting place, the sun glimmered off of its shiny metal covering. His mother and father at his sides, Mick stood quietly until his legs could no longer hold his weight. He tightly clinched their fingers as each held an arm to keep him from falling. The last words were spoken and Mick's slow tears rolled down his cheeks as he just stood there. The rest of the grieving crowd passed by and dropped red roses onto the top of the white casket as they returned to their cars. Fixated on the grave and gasping for air through a choking voice no one else could hear, Mick exhaled the words "I love you" then turned and walked away.

Shrieks from the alarm clock pierced the morning air and the display read

6:15 AM as Mick laid on the bed staring at the ceiling. He had been doing this on and off for the last six or seven hours. Every time he closed his eyes he saw Sarah's face. Sometimes he saw her silky skin and alluring eyes, other times he was horrified by the sight of the blood which ran down Sarah's face just after the car bomb exploded, moments before she gasped her last breath.

The bed was a rock and he twisted and twirled under the sheets hour after hour trying to shake the images to no avail. It was better just to keep his eyes open. Still, he couldn't help but stare at her empty pillow. Finally, the sun was up. He sat straight up and put his feet on the floor to begin his journey back to sanity. Amazingly, he was not tired. He was probably still in shock and, at the very least, in need of some psychological counseling. His parents had urged him to see someone – just to talk. There was no way he would. Mick was determined to get through this ordeal in his own way. His eight o'clock class would be the first step. He got in the shower and managed to wash his hair and face without once closing his eyes. Driving to campus with a cup of hot coffee wedged between his legs, as he always did, gave him his first sense of normalcy in just over three weeks. Mick had been ready to go back to work a week after Sarah died; however, the Dean had insisted that he take another two week sabbatical. Rather than argue, Mick did what he was told.

The story of Sarah being murdered while the newlyweds honeymooned in Ireland had been all over the local newspapers. The college paper, the Chamberlain University Press, had run a front page piece. Most of the students didn't know what to say as they trickled into Mick's classroom, so most said nothing. Two female students stopped by the podium where he was reviewing his lesson plan and offered brief words of condolence. "Sorry for your loss, Mr. McKenna," one said. He'd heard it hundreds of times at the funeral home. It was kind of the girls nonetheless. He just smiled and said thank you.

Mick began the lecture on *New York Times v. Sullivan*, a famous libel case, the same way he always did. But this time something was different. Suddenly, he remembered that this was the very classroom where he had first met Sarah. This unnerved him in a way that he did not expect. He couldn't concentrate. The room seemed small and his words echoed off the concrete walls. As he looked from his lesson plan into the crowd before him, every eye was like a laser pointed directly at his face. He looked down at his papers and continued on.

The room began to close in around him and he felt his heart begin to beat out of his chest. As he yammered on, beads of sweat formed on his forehead and slowly dripped over his eyebrows. To keep from becoming completely unglued, he stopped and turned his back to the class to take a sip of coffee, along with a few deep breaths to keep from hyperventilating. This had never happened to him before and he didn't know if he was having a heart attack or if he was just freaking out. He turned around and there, right in the first row, was Sarah looking up at him just like she did the first day he had laid eyes on her. Startled, his head jerked back. He blinked and blinked through his sweat soaked eyes until she was gone and the face of a real live student snapped him back into reality. Mick rubbed his face and eyes harshly, exhaled, and involuntarily released the death grip he had on his coffee cup. The steaming black liquid covered the floor. He calmly said, "Excuse me class," and walked out, shutting the door quietly behind him. The students sat there stunned.

The moment the door shut, Mick sprinted down the hallway, out the double doors into the parking lot, and ran all the way to his car. When he stopped running he caught his breath and immediately started to cry harder than he had ever cried in his life. He hadn't cried like this the entire time Sarah had been dead. He cried to the point of sobbing and once the tears finally stopped falling, he wiped his face and nose with his sleeve, took a deep breath, got in his car and started driving. Apparently, his return *had* been too soon.

Mick's passport was still valid so getting on an international flight would be easy. He had driven around and around the city for over three hours, in a trance, thinking more than driving.

Emptiness consumed him. He was confused but a vaguely developing urge kept creeping into his mind – one that he couldn't explain. Mick didn't stop driving until he figured out his next move. He stopped at the apartment, made a call to the airline, wrote a short letter to the University accepting the Dean's previous offer to let a substitute finish out the semester, and dialed his father's number, hoping to get the answering machine so he could just leave a message.

"You've reached the McKenna's, we can't get to the phone right now, please leave a message and we'll call you right back. Thanks," his Mother's voice said followed by a long beep.

"Hi Mom, Hi Dad," Mick said in the most upbeat voice he could muster, "I'm taking a few weeks off. I'm going on a short trip and I'll be back soon. I'll give you a call in a little bit. Love you guys. Talk to you later."

Mick grabbed the same honeymoon suitcase that he never had the nerve to unpack. He left Sarah's suitcase untouched. He'd never had the courage to unpack her things. He removed a plastic bag of dirty clothes from his case and threw it onto the bed, leaving only the clean clothes he never had a chance to wear once the honeymoon was cut short. He didn't care what was in the bag – as long as he had something to wear once he landed. He grabbed the same carryon bag he and Sarah had used on their honeymoon and drove south on I-95 towards Philadelphia International. USAir flight 883 to Belfast's Aldergrove Airport was leaving the United States in less than two hours and Mick McKenna would be on it.

He had no idea why.

Chapter 2

THREE AIRPLANE BOTTLES of whiskey later and forty minutes into the flight, Mick finally relaxed and began to sink into his window seat. As his eyes glazed over and he stared at the puffy clouds below, he drifted off into a day dream about the Irish honeymoon he and Sarah had embarked on just six weeks earlier. As Mick's eyes grew heavy and the Jameson took hold, he could see vividly the brown and tan outline of Quinn's Bed and Breakfast, just fifteen miles outside of Dublin, where they stayed the first night. He fumbled through his carryon bag and found Sarah's daily planner. The leather bound case which Sarah usually kept in her pocketbook smelled of her perfume. Mick closed his eyes and held the book up to his nose, sniffing in her sweet memory. As he closed his eyes from exhaustion and drifted into a full blown dream, he saw Sarah walk across the room in her bathrobe.

The new Mr. and Mrs. McKenna stood in front of the room's oversized picture window, snuggling, taking in the beauty that is Ireland. As they looked out at the forty shades of green countryside stretched for miles before them, Mick opened Sarah's robe and caressed her bare stomach. Although he would never know it, his unborn daughter rested comfortably in his bride's womb.

A talking head on the television, with a heavy British accent, prattled on about the shooting death of an IRA volunteer four days earlier in West Belfast. Political leaders weighed in on the effect of the murder on the peace talks currently underway in Northern Ireland. The consensus was that if the Catholics and Protestants continued to kill each other, "the Troubles" in Northern Ireland would never end. The McKenna's never heard a word of it.

What would prove to be an unforgettable honeymoon began in Dublin. Without the restraints of a formalized tour group, Mick and Sarah lazily ambled around the south of Ireland for ten days, their tour books proving to be excellent guides. They enjoyed Dublin Castle, St Patrick's Cathedral, the Custom House, and Trinity College, where they were mesmerized by the beautiful ornate script and calligraphy of the Book of Kells. In the nearby village of Slane, they ate authentic Irish scone and visited the Hill of Tara, the ancient seat of the high Kings of Ireland. On an amazing Georgian style street, smack in the middle of Dublin, Mick stumbled upon the James Joyce Center and spent hours speaking to the direct descendants of Joyce and gazing at artifacts used by the artist himself.

They rented a Ford Escort and drove to Butler Castle and St. Canice's Cathedral in Kilkenny. They were awed by the world renowned Crystal Factory in Waterford, and passed on kissing the Blarney Stone after a bartender in Cork let it slip that the local teenagers liked to urinate on the famous rock at night, unbeknownst to the puckering tourists. They toured the Ring of Kerry, the Lakes of Killarney and the spectacular views of the Atlantic near Moll's Gap. Their exploration of the south of Ireland came to a close with an exhilarating, and at times dangerous, stroll along the windy and mind-blowing Cliffs of Moher, in County Clare. The North of Ireland would be next. They considered heading to either Londonderry or Belfast. They decided to simply drive north without a destination for the time being and pick one later.

On a small twisty country road, in a town neither could find on their map, they came around a bend and were suddenly mobbed by a flock of sheep who had decided to camp out on the narrow road. An old farmer, at least seventy-five years old, smiled a gaunt, toothless smile, tipped his paddy cap, and waved good morning as eighty or ninety sheep bleated and bayed their way around the shiny Ford, taking their time to get from the pasture on the left side of the road to the pasture on the right. Neither the farmer nor the sheep were in any hurry. Every few minutes a stray would veer down the road instead of crossing it and the skinny old farmer, in his hip high waders, slowly waltzed after each, welcoming the wandering soul back to the fold with a gentle nudge of his walking stick. Time stood still there and Mick and Sarah giggled as they wallowed in a woolen traffic jam in a world that was vastly different than the workday world that was slowly but surely withering away in their memories. After the sheep cleared, they drove around the bend and stopped at a crossroads. The signs pointed left to Londonderry, right to Belfast. Mick looked at Sarah and shrugged his shoulders, "You pick." Sarah looked down at her tour books – neither had any information on the North. She twirled the books playfully into the back seat and said, "I guess we'll wing it from here. Belfast sounds good to me – make a right."

Belfast was much more of a big city than they expected. They arrived in the early morning and the streets were full of people working and shopping in the City Center, unlike the tourist crowds normally found in the more popular Dublin. This was the hustle and bustle of a large European city. The city was old and beautiful. Sarah enjoyed the fact that they were discovering the city on their own – without a tour guide or a book. As they wandered the city, everything they found was more exciting and special. They went to High Street, St. George's Market, Albert Clock, and even drove out to the wharf in Belfast where the Titanic was fitted with its heavy superstructure. Next was lunch at a local bar and a tour of City Hall.

In a comfortable booth in a small warm corner of the Old Antrim Pub on Donegall Place, a light rain trickled down the window pane next to Mick and Sarah. Mick never tasted fish and chips as good. Flakey, lightly breaded Atlantic Cod alongside a tray full of French fried potato slices as thick as thumbs. Sarah was picking at her lamb chop and soda bread.

"What's wrong?" Mick said, "Aren't you hungry?"

Sarah scrunched up her lips and rolled her eyes, "I'm just a little queasy. It's probably from the Guinness you forced me to try last night," she said, then smiled across at him.

Mick laughed and harpooned a triangle of soda bread from her plate. She shook her head as the bread disappeared into his jowls.

Outside a crowd was forming along the sidewalks of the street that lead towards Belfast City Hall. Sarah's natural nosiness was peaked as she peered out from behind the dark walnut window sill. She could hear music – bagpipes?

"What's going on out there?" she muttered.

Before Mick could answer, she was pulling on her jacket and grabbed for her camera bag. Mick didn't try to stop her. Sarah's journalistic juices were flowing and he knew that he would soon be left behind. She looked back at him, devilishly, half seeking approval as she slung her Nikon F-4 around her neck. "Go ahead," he said with his crooked smile, "I'll get the check and meet you out front."

Sarah stepped up behind the crowd and looked to her right. The rain slowed to a drizzle. The wide Belfast sidewalks closer to City Hall were packed with hundreds of mourners and observers crammed shoulder to shoulder. Out in the center of the road, a priest in gold and purple robes led a funeral procession. Traffic had been stopped by the police and three alter boys in simple black cloaks and white ropes tied around their waists walked behind a long ornate staff which held a pewter crucifix at least seven foot high. Straight behind, a simple wooden coffin, draped in the Irish Tricolor flag, rested atop the shoulders of six burley men in black suits walking in lock step down the street, which she now saw was lined with yellow barricades and a multitude of onlookers. A bagpiper in full Scottish regalia, including a kilt, followed the coffin. She squeezed off a few broad, initial shots with her camera. Another crowd, at least two hundred strong, turned the nearby corner and marched somberly behind the bagpipes. The rain turned to a fog-like mist as Sarah stood quietly and listened. She had never heard Amazing Grace on the bagpipes before – it was eerie but beautiful.

Suddenly, Sarah heard the clicking sound of metal and the hum of huge tires gripping the wet roadway. Four British foot soldiers, carrying M-16's and wearing bullet proof vests and combat helmets, escorted a Saracen tank as it turned out of an alley and crawled down the street behind the procession. The soldiers turned and walked backwards every ten steps, then spun and scanned the street and crowd left and right before walking forward again, looking intently for anything out of place or suspicious. A Gatlin gun was mounted on the top of the tank and the soldier whose torso was sticking out the hole on the top of the tank seemed ready to fire on command. Two more soldiers stood in the bed of an open back Range Rover jeep, holding their weapons high as the armed driver lead the way.

The sight of a tank in the middle of an urban setting following closely behind a funeral procession was riveting to Sarah but no one in the crowd seemed phased at all – British occupation had been a reality for the people of Northern Ireland for almost a quarter century.

She fired off nearly an entire roll of film on the tank, the soldiers, and the accepting faces of the regular citizens. She had been hoping to get some shots of the occupational forces if she and Mick went up North. She knew a little bit about "the Troubles" going on in Belfast and she had been hoping to take some photographs of the soldiers juxtaposed against the life of the ordinary people. That was the real reason she wanted to go to the North but she never mentioned her reasoning or the on-going troubles to Mick. He would have wanted to steer clear even though the conflict had been quiet here in recent years. She took close ups of the soldiers faces which all seemed to be so young and baby faced. One of the soldiers even gave her a nervous smile for the camera.

The parade stopped momentarily as the priest said a prayer. Sarah reloaded the camera on the fly as she moved down the street, back towards the front of the procession. The fact that she was on vacation was irrelevant – she was in full work mode now.

The sight of a wooden coffin held high in the middle of a crowded street triggered a memory of the Ayatollah Khomeini's funeral in Sarah's head. She had seen the blurry images of the frenzied Iranian crowd on TV a decade earlier when she was thirteen. Eight people were crushed to death in the throng's fanatical quest to kiss the dead body of the Iranian leader. Suddenly, the horrifying image of the Ayatollah's coffin being jostled by the crazed mob until the corpse bounced out, barefoot, onto the street flashed in her head. Surely, the corpse in front of her now would not end up in the street.

"Whose funeral is this?" she asked an elderly woman standing near the curb.

The woman turned her twisted torso, "This is the great volunteer Brian Bethan," she said, kissing the rosary wrapped around her seemingly crippled hand as she blessed herself and turned back toward the spectacle.

"What sort of volunteer?" Sarah asked.

"IRA, what else?" the old woman said as she turned away again with a puzzled look. The growing murmur of the crowd, roar of the tank, and the squeals of the bagpipes had apparently masked Sarah's American accent.

The funeral parade began to move slowly. Sarah progressed down the street with the coffin and stood back on a stoop to snap a few shots. She needed to get closer. The mass of humanity was becoming greater and greater the closer she got to City Hall. She saw the first political signs and squeezed into the middle of the crowd which was now about six deep and just seconds from spilling over the barricades into the street. More British foot soldiers stood inside the police barricades, armed and at the ready. About thirty police officers also lined the street in an effort to control the swelling crowd. The air within the crush of people was no longer cold. Sarah felt the immense body heat of hundreds of human beings and the initial sway of the crushing mob. It was hard to breathe. The smell of wet clothes hung in the air. The bag pipes were soon drowned out by the chanting voices. In all the commotion it was barely discernable, but there appeared to be two factions:

"England out of Ireland, now," chanted one faction;

"God save the Queen," came the retort from the other side of the street.

Mick walked out of the pub. Sarah was not outside the building. He looked to his left, and then his right. After seeing the full extent of the spectacle they had only had a glimpse of from inside the pub, he was not surprised. He knew Sarah would be in the thick of it. The crowd was deep and noisy. Mick jumped up in the air several times trying to spy her green jacket in the sea of black and grey overcoats when he saw the soldiers and the tank. *What the hell is going on here?* he thought.

    Sarah squeezed under the elbows of two huge men, and squirted beyond the barricade out behind a rusty blue Toyota Celica. She was out in the clear now and could breathe more easily. She was crouched less than six inches from the C-4 plastic explosives packet, tucked neatly under the wheel well of the Toyota, as she focused her lens on the unruly politicos on the other side of the street. Her camera's shutter clicked and blazed off twenty high speed shots and she pulled another roll of film to reload. The policemen lining the streets were standing with outstretched arms desperately trying to delay the inevitable discharge of the protestors and mourners into the streets. The soldiers were facing the crowd. The horde on Sarah's side of the street broke free to fall in behind the funeral parade and Sarah was quickly surrounded by people again. She saw fear in the eyes of the young soldier standing on the other side of the street. He couldn't have been more than eighteen years old and certainly didn't look liked he wanted to be there. Sarah stood up and started to inch away from the car.

The sound of the car bomb detonating and the screams that followed were surreal and deafening. Mick immediately panicked and started running frantically in the direction of the blast shouting her name. Running toward him with looks of horror were people covered in blood and soot. Flames were shooting through the cloud of smoke ahead. He was knocked down twice by the fleeing mob on his way towards the flaming, burnt out car. A woman holding a child in one arm stood and screamed something over and over again but the words were warbled as Mick raced by her. A young soldier grabbed his arm as he got close, pulling at his coat, warning him to get back. Mick pushed him hard in the chest and the soldier released his grip with an astonished look as Mick broke free. The air smelled like fire. He ran as fast as he could but still felt like he was running in the slow motion of a dream. Mick stopped as he reached the opening in the crowd, just seconds after the explosion. His eyes were tearing from the smoke and fear. It was hard to see. He scanned the street, then the sidewalks. She was not there. He turned in almost a complete circle. Sarah was nowhere to be found. He began to feel a sense of relief – then he saw it. In between two cars parked on the other side of the road. The green jacket. Sarah's green jacket.

Sarah was laying face down about twenty feet from the car. In an instance, his intestines sank in his stomach and he broke into a cold sweat. Mick sprinted to her side, dropped to his knees and carefully rolled her over, fearing what he was about to see. Her eyes were closed, her face was covered in blood. Her body was limp and lifeless. For a moment he thought she might still be alive. He shook her and called her name. She did not respond. Then he saw the gaping wound in the side of her head and the enormous puddle of crimson blood surrounding them.

She was not breathing. Her skin was still warm. There was no pulse. No life. No Sarah. She was gone.

Chapter 3

SPECIAL AGENT CECIL MAXWELL pulled the Venetian blinds down to cut the glare of the New York City sunlight beaming through his office window as he hunched over in his chair, flipping through the four inch thick surveillance report. On the cover of the brown file jacket the name OPERATION EMERALD – SECURITY LEVEL THREE was stamped in red ink. The loud ring from the phone made him jump.

"Special Agent Maxwell," he said still glued to the report.

"It's Jensen," the voice on the other line said, "You should come down here. Looks like our friends are getting busy again."

"Where are you?" Maxwell asked.

"Port of Brooklyn, Pier 19. Customs just raided a container headed for Belfast and let's just say, based on what we just found, the IRA isn't exactly ready to be put out to pasture. These Customs agents don't know what to do and are getting antsy. They want to call NYPD."

"Don't let them do anything or talk to anyone. I'll be right there," said Maxwell as he slammed down the receiver and bounded out the door into the elevator.

Maxwell had been with the FBI for twelve years since leaving the New York Police Department after a stellar but brief career. He came from a long line of tough Brooklyn cops, he and his two brothers following in the footsteps of their father and grandfather. Ever since he was a boy, Maxwell knew what he wanted to do. His uncle John was killed on a street corner while on the job – shot in the head in broad daylight. The thug who pulled the trigger was a sixteen year old kid, high on crack, with no idea that Uncle John was a police officer and no idea why he felt compelled to put three slugs of lead through his skull. At his sentencing hearing the crack head simply guessed, "It was the drugs." Maxwell was ten years old at the time and vowed that someday he would work to get trash like that off the streets. He took the department's entrance exam two weeks out of high school. He scored in the top quarter of all applicants but languished on the waiting list for two years before he was accepted into the academy because of all the affirmative action candidates in line before him. It wasn't fair, but he waited patiently nonetheless.

The family and the force had high expectations when Cecil Maxwell graduated first in his class at the academy. However, his career had a rocky start. Three months into his rookie assignment to the 51st Precinct up in Harlem, he stumbled upon evidence that his partner, Nick Deluca, a twenty year veteran of the force, was shaking down drug dealers in exchange for looking the other way while they pushed their junk in the neighborhoods. Maxwell was a boy scout of sorts and there was no way he could ignore a dirty cop on the take. Hell, this was the very thing that he had just dedicated his life to stopping and this scum bag was making a living off of it.

He watched Deluca carefully for two months, documenting everything. Deluca appeared to know Maxwell was onto him but didn't seem to care a bit. The whole thing had obviously been going on for many years in front of a number of past partners who dared not speak up. Maxwell knew all too well that that cops generally protect their own, so he knew it would be professional suicide to go to Internal Affairs. He did it anyway. When Maxwell testified against him, Deluca threatened to kill him from the defense table. With the evidence Maxwell collected, the district attorney won an easy conviction, Deluca lost his job and pension, and was sentenced to twenty years in the Elmira Correctional Facility in upstate New York. Some good cops who worked with his Uncle John and his Dad assured Maxwell that he had done the right thing and told him to hang in there – the City needed more cops like him. However, most of the cops in the precinct had a different take on things. The majority steered clear of him; others made snide comments.

Three weeks after the trial, Maxwell was sitting on a bench in the locker room, bent down, putting on his socks after a hot shower at the change of shifts. Hugo Rivera, a six foot four, three hundred and twenty pound Spanish hulk of a cop walked in and immediately gave him the same dirty look he had been giving him at shift change ever since Maxwell turned in Deluca. Maxwell just looked away. Rivera had been trying to start something and Maxwell would not give him the satisfaction. Hugo couldn't keep it to hard looks – not any more. He walked over and with one of his massive hands slammed a locker door shut.

"Why the hell don't you just get the fuck out of here?" he said, "Nobody needs your kind here."

"And what kind is that?" asked Maxwell with a smart tone.

"You know what you are. You messed with a man's livelihood. You have no fucking business wearing that badge."

Maxwell stood up.

"You have no idea what you are talking about Hugo. You don't know a thing about me; you don't know a thing about Deluca."

Maxwell was getting louder.

"Just let it go, let it go," he said, trying but failing to keep his cool.

"You're a piece of shit...," Hugo said as he got closer to Maxwell's face.

His eyes bulged with surprise when Maxwell reached up, wrapped his hand around the larger man's throat, slamming the back of his head hard against the locker. Within two seconds Hugo's windpipe was blocked and he became paralyzed with fear. Maxwell squeezed for a few more seconds. He knew that with one move he could take the fat bastard's life. Rivera was no better than the dirt bag Maxwell had just sent to prison. He considered choking him out right there but it just wasn't worth it. Maxwell released the grip on the Adam's apple. He had proven his point. Hugo slid off the locker, grabbed his own throat with both hands, rubbed it, coughed and spit, then leaned forward, close enough for Maxwell to smell the garlic emanating from the pit of his stomach, and blurted, "You're nothing but a fucking rat!" and walked away knowing full well that he no longer wanted any piece of Officer Cecil Maxwell.

No one wanted to be partnered with a rat who would watch their every move, so the Captain, who was none too pleased about the disgrace that had befallen his station house, moved Maxwell from "last out" (the midnight to eight a.m. shift) to day shift, where it was much safer to drive alone in Harlem. He worked alone for a year and a half and made more drugs and weapons possessions arrests than any duo in any precinct in any of New York's five boroughs. The Captain of Internal Affairs had Maxwell on his radar as a potential new recruit ever since he came forward about Deluca and was impressed with his arrest record. Most of the detectives in Internal Affairs had at one time turned somebody in. Maxwell was tinkering with the idea of entering law school and a potential career as a prosecutor when he was approached regarding his willingness to transfer to Internal Affairs as a full detective. He thought about it for exactly one minute and then jumped at the opportunity. It was the one place he knew he would not be expected to accept corruption. He spent three years at Internal Affairs where he quickly became an expert in surveillance and covert investigation. In that time, he married Laura, who he had been dating since high school and they had a son, Brody.

In his last year at Internal Affairs, during a drug sting involving a ring of dirty cops and some Jamaican drug lords up in Harlem, Maxwell coordinated with a federal agent in the FBI's drug task force, Special Agent Dalton Briggs. Briggs and he pulled a few all night surveillance details and hit if off like old friends. Briggs was a cop's cop but was also clean as a whistle, just like Maxwell. Briggs explained in detail how the FBI was a perfect fit and they talked about Maxwell jumping ship to work with the feds. Being squeaky clean and straight as a boy scout were the qualities the FBI searched high and low for, qualities that were hard to find, even in good cops. Before long Maxwell climbed into his Honda Accord and took the first of many seven hour drives to FBI Headquarters in Quantico, Virginia for an interview.

The background checks, polygraph, exhausting physical tests, and grueling psychological interviews were tough but Maxwell had been up to the task and was accepted into the FBI Academy. After four months of intensive tactical, behavioral, operational, and forensic training, followed by a mind blowing battery of physical, written, and oral exams, Cecil Maxwell was a Special Agent in the Federal Bureau of Investigation. He was initially assigned to Dalton's drug task force and quickly rose up the ranks. The work was similar to the work he did on the street as a detective. His street sense was highly evolved and everyone deferred to his hunches when he had them because he was almost always right. Crack and cocaine were rampant, the drugs of choice in the eighties, and together Maxwell and Briggs put a hurting on the ability of drug traffickers to get their product supplied and distributed in not only New York but in the entire Northeastern United States. Their work lead to a series of high profile federal racketeering prosecutions, which ensnared Columbians working out of Texas and Florida and their Mafioso counterparts on the East coast. The two were a team of star Feds who the United States Attorneys relied upon heavily. Briggs was sad to see his protégé go but, after eight years, a promotion for Maxwell was unavoidable and he was given his own unit inside the Western Europe Counter Terrorism Division.

The new post sounded much sexier than it was. During the late seventies and eighties, the Western Europe Counter Terrorism Division had been a hot bed of activity while gun running from various big cities up and down the Eastern seaboard to the Irish Republican Army in Northern Ireland was in full effect. However, peace had been on the horizon in Ireland since the mid-nineties. Gun running had all but stopped from the United States and, as a result, this division was a safe place to put a new unit leader. There were still suspects to watch and leads to run down; however, the job was to be a quiet learning ground where Maxwell could hone his craft for about five years and learn to be a high level Special Agent in Charge, managing other Special Agents without much pressure from the Director, or any of the other government agencies that routinely exerted pressure on FBI resources. And a quiet learning ground it had been. Until now.

Jensen's phone call that morning would prove to be the calm before the storm. Earlier in the day, a U.S. Customs officer conducting a routine check in the marine terminal at the Port of Brooklyn ordered the opening of seventeen rented shipping containers supposed to be full of furniture and vehicles en route via cargo ship to Dublin, Ireland. In the eighth container they opened, the agents unearthed a cache of sixty AK-47 assault rifles and a dozen crates full of hand grenades also made by the Russians.

Maxwell's black Crown Victoria kicked up dusty asphalt as he screeched to a stop at the Port of Brooklyn dockside where he found Jensen talking with two agents from Customs. He motioned for Jensen to come over to the car and inside he briefed Maxwell concisely, as he had been taught, regarding what was found and where the shipment was headed. Jensen explained that the invoice from the container company indicated it was rented by a Sean Ryan who left his Bronx apartment two weeks ago and got on a plane to Dublin to eagerly await the arrival of his assault weapons and grenades, which were described as "furniture and household items" in the inventory section of the rental invoice.

Jensen's team had already determined that Sean Ryan was a bogus name but the address he gave was real. An hour earlier Jensen's partner had visited the clerk at the front desk/rental office of the dumpy apartment building and confirmed that the guy in apartment 4C, rented in the name of Sean Ryan, pretty much kept to himself, had an Irish accent, stayed for about a month and then just disappeared one day. The clerk dug around and found a photo copy of a New York State driver's license Ryan had produced in order to complete the apartment rental application. The FBI computers confirmed in minutes that the New York State Department of Motor Vehicles never issued the license and had no record of this Sean Ryan. One phone call to JFK airport confirmed the name Sean Ryan appearing on an Aer Lingus flight manifest fourteen days earlier. Maxwell knew that Sean Ryan, or whoever he was, was gone.

Even so, Maxwell had a plan to find him.

After a few minutes Maxwell got out of the car, walked over to the Customs agents, flashed his badge and asked, "FBI. Who's in charge here?"

"I'm Special Agent in Charge, Lance Popson," responded the smaller blond haired Customs agent.

"This case is now under the jurisdiction of the FBI. We are taking over the investigation and we're letting this container head out to its destination," Maxwell said boldly, with a tone of finality.

"You've got to be kidding me. This was our find," Popson said angrily.

"This is clearly our jurisdiction. There's an on-going investigation into illegal shipments from the States to Dublin. We've been tracking this for eighteen months," concealing his blatant lie with an air of confidence.

In actuality, the FBI hadn't had a lead on an arms shipment to Ireland in over three years. All of the bugged phone lines and snooping on in-person conversations between their usual suspects had brought forth nothing because apparently nothing had been going on. This was merely a lucky break for Maxwell and his unit.

Maxwell continued, "Look, we are going to leave the weapons on the container, put them on the ship, and nail whoever picks it up on the other side. After the bust, we'll give you the weapons – then you can grab all the glory you want, OK? But for now, this is how it is going to be."

Popson just shook his head and walked away. There was no use fighting. The FBI always got what it wanted.

Chapter 4

MICK TORE THE PAGE from Sarah's daily planner and began frantically walking up and down the streets of Belfast for hours. Finally, in the area known as The Market, he looked up from his twisted page and saw the door with the address he had been looking for – number 14 Ormeau Road.

Mick had found the address in Sarah's daily planner. Sarah had done some rough genealogical research before their trip so that they could visit a distant relative of the McKenna clan while they were on their honeymoon. Mick recalled thinking the connection between the McKenna's and the O'Neils was very loose and quite questionable when Sarah told him about her research. She just laughed and told him it would be "fun" to stop in for a visit.

Mick nervously knocked at the door. Getting no answer he knocked harder and harder and still there was no answer. "Three thousand miles for this – nobody home!" he thought. Mick leaned over the railing to peer through the small gap in the lace curtains that hung from the window. Suddenly, the door swung open, producing a somewhat worn woman in her fifties with a head of gray hair that looked like straw.

"Mrs. O'Neil?" Mick asked stepping back onto the stoop.

"Yes?" she responded.

"I wonder if I could talk to your husband for a moment?"

"Surely, what's this about? You're an American, are you not?" asked Mrs. O'Neil.

"Yes, I am – my name is Mick McKenna. I think I'm related to your husband and I need to talk to him."

Although a stranger, Mick was well-dressed and harmless – she could tell he was a bit lost and invited him in.

"Tommy! There's somebody here to see you!" she bellowed with a voice much rougher that the sweet one she used at the door.

"I'll be right there," yelled big Tom O'Neil.

"Would you like a cup of tea?" asked his wife as she turned into the kitchen leaving Mick in the parlor.

"Thank you," Mick replied.

As Mick sat waiting in the parlor, he looked around the room. He could not help to think how odd it was to see pictures of Jesus, Pope John Paul II and President John F. Kennedy displayed together so neatly over the tiny fire place, alongside a picture of a beautiful young girl. The small fire burning in the hearth made the room nice and warm. On the table next to him sat wedding invitation, memorialized forever in a small picture frame. Mick held it in his hands as thoughts of his life with Sarah started to swirl.

Mick and Sarah's life together began four years earlier. He was a second-year assistant professor at Chamberlain University, just outside of Philadelphia. She was a journalism student with no real interest in Communications Law but had taken the University's course on the subject nonetheless because she had an elective to fill and because she heard the professor gave an easy final exam.
 The romance started slowly during the fall semester in 1994. Mick noticed

her on the first day. While all the college girls tried hard to look good by piling on tons of makeup and wearing tight, all too revealing clothes, Sarah was dressed in a simple pair of comfortable khaki shorts, an oversized tie-dyed t-shirt and sandals. Even in such loose fitting clothes her long tan legs and feminine curves caught Mick's attention and stood out in the crowd. During the first few weeks of class, he would often find himself lecturing from whatever side of the room gave him the best view of her. Her hair was straight, shoulder length and light blonde. She was very understated but not shy. Her soft hazel eyes, with not a hint of makeup, drew him to her at first. More than once, Sarah caught his stare linger a little bit too long and, after a while, she knew he was interested. Sarah was the one to strike up the first conversation. Although she knew that Chamberlain faculty members were forbidden from dating students, she was compulsively drawn by Mick's strong but gentlemanly way. Her attraction to him had also been immediate. His tall athletic build, thick chest and crooked smile – she couldn't stop staring at him at times. Ever the aggressive one, it was all she could do to force herself to wait until the semester was just about over before approaching him. He responded to her invitation to meet "off campus" without hesitation.

Their first contact outside of the class room was unnecessarily shrouded in secrecy. They met at a café eight miles from the university. The café started out as the place they would meet and talk, grew into the place where they confided in one another and became friends, and ended up being the place where they first kissed. Before long they realized that as long as they were not seen on campus holding hands and kissing like hormonal teenagers no one would know their secret, so they didn't try hard to conceal their interest in one another. Who really would have cared anyway – they were both adults. They saw each other a few times a week at first and eventually spent just about every night and every weekend together. They fell in love as the semester changed from winter to spring.

From the beginning, Sarah saw something extremely masculine in Mick but he had tenderness at the same time. She was twenty three and he was only a few years older. He was dry and funny, yet he had a maturity and kindness that she had never known in a man even close to her age.

They waited until April – three months – before spending their first night together. When they finally did, the date lasted the entire Spring Break with the two only leaving bed from time to time to sneak down to the kitchen for food. The physical and emotional attachment was of a strength neither had ever felt before. From then on, they saw each other every day.

Two months later, Sarah graduated with a Journalism degree and the Monday after Commencement she moved her clothes and books into Mick's apartment. She quickly found a job as a part time reporter and photographer at a small local community newspaper. Every day Mick raced home from work in his beaten up Toyota Camry to see this beautiful woman who had miraculously come into his life. They lived in a small one bedroom apartment ten minutes from campus. The place was a dump but they didn't care. They were living on a teacher's salary and whatever Sarah could bring home for each picture she took and story she wrote. Mick worked at becoming a full professor, while Sarah strove to land a job with one of the big Philadelphia newspapers. Until then, they had decided to live a meager life. The plan was to work hard, get their careers on track, buy a house, and start a family. They talked about getting married but decided to wait until they could afford to do it right. Mick worked diligently researching and writing papers for publication in academic journals – the shortest route to becoming a tenured professor. Sarah picked up as many freelance jobs as she could find.

Sarah's career as a journalist quickly evolved into that of a photojournalist, based largely on her keen eye and aggressive attitude. After two and a half years of hardnosed local paper grunt work, she was the first reporter on the scene of a balcony collapse at a ritzy hotel on the Philadelphia side of the Delaware River. The balcony was part of an outdoor night club and her photographs of the rescue workers' lifesaving efforts were plastered all over the front pages of the Philadelphia Inquirer and the Philadelphia Daily News. She had climbed out onto the maintenance track hanging under the nearby Benjamin Franklin Bridge and, while risking her own life, was able to take shots that no other reporter could get near. The owners of the nightclub were sued in a highly publicized seven week trial and every other day another one of her photographs was on the front page. Eventually, the news editor at the Inquirer turned sick of paying her suddenly in demand freelance fees and decided to hire her full time. She had made it. The day she came home and told Mick the good news, he emptied their paltry savings account, took her to their favorite little Italian restaurant in South Philadelphia to celebrate, dropped to one knee and pulled his grandmother's engagement ring from his pocket. As Mick knelt before her they both laughed as a corny accordion player with a marinara stained apron filled the air with cliché music. Sarah sat and cried for what seemed to be five minutes without even responding to Mick's question about becoming his wife. No response was needed. They both knew the answer.

A large man, about the same age as Mrs. O'Neil with a protruding belly and an unruly head of whitish hair bounced down the stairs and filled up the doorway, as Mick looked up and hurriedly slid the framed invite back onto the side table. Stepping into the parlor, the man's largeness seemed to shrink the size of the already tiny room.

"Tom O'Neil," the immense man said, "What can I do for you?" extending a hand as big and as rough as a shovel.

"Well, Mr. O'Neil, I don't know exactly where to begin...." Mick started.

He began by explaining the scattered family tree that seemed to indicate a relationship between his family and the O'Neils. He explained that his wife had written the address in her daily planner thinking that maybe they might pay a visit when they were in Ireland. Then suddenly he found himself beginning to tell the story of his wife's death for the first time. He started with the honeymoon, went on to the bomb blast, the coroner, and the murder investigation, explained the trip back home, then the funeral, and ended up with his class room freak out and unplanned hop on an airliner across the Atlantic to their front door. O'Neil listened intently – he had been working in the section of town where the car bomb exploded that day and recalled that the only person killed was an American woman. Mrs. O'Neil, entering with the tea, realized the seriousness of the conversation and sat quietly as Mick stumbled through the difficult recollection.

"Mr....."

"...McKenna," Mick interjected.

"Mr. McKenna, we're awfully sorry to hear about your wife – but what exactly can we do for you?" Tom O'Neil asked, careful not to appear too cold.

"I don't even know myself...I guess I was hoping you could help me understand how all of this happened.... I know you have no idea who I am and I don't even know if we're really related – but yours was the only name I knew in this entire country and I had to start somewhere."

Mick's insides began to rumble, his heart started to beat hard, and the room started to close in on him again, as he suddenly realized how insane he must have been to barge his way into the home of two complete strangers and ask them to help him piece together the craziness that had become his life. Obviously upset, Mick fumbled for his coat, awkwardly set down his teacup, almost knocked the lid off the ceramic tea pot Mrs. O'Neil had set on the table, and headed toward the door apologizing.

"Listen, this is crazy, I'm sorry. Thank you. I'm sorry for bothering you," he said.

Mrs. O'Neil, could see her visitor was frazzled and in need of a bit of comfort. She commanded, in a way only a mother could, "No, no, no, no. Listen here, there's no family member of mine coming all the way to Ireland and not staying for dinner."

"No, thank you, please, I wouldn't want to impose," Mick responded.

"Mr. McKenna, you wouldn't want to offend me now would you?" she replied with a disapproving look, then a smile.

Mick began to relax, and having nowhere else to go and no other plan, reluctantly replied, "Okay then, I'll stay. Thank you...thank you very much."

"Tommy, why don't you boys go and have a wee drink while I get the dinner on," she ordered.

Big Tom was shocked that he was actually being told to drink but he wasn't about to look a gift horse in the mouth. He obediently pulled on his cap and coat and answered, "Yes, love – see you in an hour."

The night air was cool and Mick could see his breath before him as O'Neil offered him a cigarette. They walked the three blocks to Macquire's Public House without a saying word – each man enjoying his smoke. The pub was nestled on the corner of a dark street. A green neon light framed the only window of the small dimly lit stone building. As the two men stepped through the doorway, the regulars huddled inside the bar's dark corners stopped their private conversations long enough to realize it was O'Neil. O'Neil seemed to nod his reassurance that the stranger with him was OK. This was a Catholic bar and only Catholics were welcome.

"Johnny, give us two pints," said O'Neil.

"Aye," said Johnny, wiping the bar.

"Well, Mick, why have you come to this God forsaken place?" the big man asked.

"I don't really know. I guess I'm here to find the man responsible for killing my wife. The police, the RUC or whatever they call them, told me that since the bomb went off at a terrorist's funeral, they can't talk to me. They said it was in the hands of their Special Investigators, that they would contact the American Consulate if they learn anything new."

"Special Investigators. Ha! Now that's a loch of bullshit! They'll say anything to protect the bastards," said O'Neil already gulping the end of his pint and motioning to Johnny for two more.

"The police will?" Mick inquired.

"Oh, you better believe it. What you don't understand is that we're in a fucking war here and the police are on their side!" O'Neil said as his face began to redden.

"Whose side?" asked Mick.

"The Brits, the orange bastards, the fucking Loyalists that set the bomb. That bomb was meant for a Republican. A member of the IRA. Did they tell you that? Your wife was just in the wrong place at the wrong time."

Mick explained, "Listen, Republicans, Loyalists? I don't know what any of it means. All I know about what's going on over here is what I've seen on TV. The Protestants and the Catholics are killing each other and the British say they're here to keep the peace. I don't give shit about any of it...all I want is the name of the man who planted that bomb and all I need you to do is point me in the right direction."

O'Neil laughed heartily at Mick's ignorance and said, "What are you gonna do, waltz into a meeting of the UVF and kill the fucker?"

Mick had no idea what the UVF was. He just stared into the bottom of his pint and muttered softly, "We'll see, we'll see."

As he stared and stared at the yellow ale, he wondered if this was why he was here.

One of morning's yellow rays cut sharply through the dusty wooden blinds, inching slowly across the sleeping face. Briefly creeping and cresting the fleshy unshaven cheek, the beam plummeted down into a wrinkled crevice, fiendishly finding its way under a clinched lid, slipping in just enough light to steal the sleep from the unsuspecting soul below.

Mick shut his eyes tightly, rolled over, then realizing the unfamiliar feeling of the blanket, sat straight up, eyes wild and wide. *Where the hell am I?* he thought for a split second. It eventually struck him that he wasn't in his own bed. Hell, he wasn't even in the United States anymore. He closed his eyes for a moment and the end of the night before rushed back into his memory bank. He remembered his trip to the bar with O'Neil and the return home afterwards. The four pints and two shots of Jameson had relaxed him enough to sleep through the night for the first time in weeks. The alcohol had also fogged his head a bit and walking back from the pub almost two hours later he had wondered what Mrs.

O'Neil meant when she told the men to be back in an hour for "bangers and mash." He had been pleasantly surprised to sit down in front of a plate packed with a fistful of plump juicy sausages, three round mounds of mashed potatoes and a saucy side of baked beans. He had been famished and the smell of the traditional Irish cuisine had reminded him quickly of Sarah and the time they had spent on their honeymoon down South.

Through his morning haze, Mick remembered that the dining room was neatly decorated and respectfully silent as the stranger, the husband, and the wife, each worked to clear the food from their plates.

Mrs. O'Neil had broken the dead air, "Where are you staying?"

"I haven't really thought about it, I guess...." Mick stammered.

"You'll be staying here the night, then," Mrs. O'Neil had said with authority. "You'll hardly be able to find a room at this time of night. You'll worry about finding a place in the morning."

Her words had hung in the air. She never looked up. Mick knew what she had just said was a statement, not a question. Mick had simply said, "Thank you, I appreciate it." Even in his half drunk, bewildered and surreal emotional state, Mick had been touched.

As he sat on the edge of the bed, squinting in the next morning's brightness, Mick was still utterly amazed by the bare human kindness of his host and hostess. It flowed so effortlessly from them to this lost soul who had shown up on their doorstep but a few hours earlier. He couldn't imagine anyone in the United States, even himself, taking in a stranger raving like a lunatic on their front step without even a second thought. Their goodness was natural like the light shed from that morning's sun and it filled the somewhat broken man with warmth.

Chapter 5

MICK'S ONE NIGHT WITH THE O'Neils easily blurred into a week. They mostly left him alone to get his thoughts together and genuinely seemed delighted to have his company for breakfast and dinner. Mick had quickly fallen into a routine of showing up at the Belfast Central Library on Royal Avenue every morning at 9:00 a.m. when the doors were opened. The library's reference section proved to be a great primer on Irish history and the conflict brewing in Northern Ireland.

On his first visit, he started by learning about the first invasion of the British in 1171 A.D. He was surprised to learn that the division among the various sects had begun over a thousand years ago and that prior to King Henry II of England, the Normans and the Vikings had also taken the land by force. He learned that throughout history the English had tried to stamp out the Irish way of life and any sense of nationalist pride. He learned of Robert the Bruce of Scotland who battled the English in his own country and then rallied the Gaelic Lords of Ireland to revolt against the Crown to regain much land that had been previously lost. He learned that the Irish culture surged in the mid 1300's when the Black Plague killed off the majority of English and Norman conquerors, most of whom lived in the large cities where the disease flourished. He learned that the English Parliament continued to attempt to crush the Irish culture and Irish heart by passing The Statutes of Kilkenny that barred Englishmen living in Ireland from marrying Irish, wearing Irish clothes, or speaking Gaelic, the Irish language. Mick also learned that despite the English attempts to cleanse the Irish from their own land, the Irish soul could not be destroyed.

Over the next few days Mick learned that King Henry VIII in the mid-1500's made Protestantism the law of the land in all countries under English rule and how the Scots, the English and the Welsh embraced the newly mandated religion, while the Irish held steadfast onto their culture and Catholic beliefs. He learned that over the following four hundred years, the Irish Catholics suffered at the hands of British Imperialism. He learned that through every century the nationalists fought hard for Irish freedom and home rule while the unionists, or loyalists as there were often called, fought to maintain the status quo and contact with Britain. He learned that Catholics were discriminated against in the work force, in land ownership, and in every socio-economic way, so of course it was they who fought for release from the English stranglehold and made up the vast majority of nationalists. Protestants were loyal to the Crown and received every conceivable benefit of their loyalty and, thus, made up the majority of the unionists.

Today, he was riveted by the accounts of the bloody Easter Rising rebellion in 1916, the Irish Republican Army's refusal to accept nothing less than complete freedom from England, and the war that raged in the South until 1921, when a peace treaty was signed. The deal, brokered by Irishman Michael Collins, created the Irish Free State, a self-governing part of Britain. As part of the bargain,

Northern Ireland could choose to succeed from the Free State, and remain part of United Kingdom. Since the majority of the heavily populated North was Protestant and favored in the English system of government, the option was quickly exercised. Thus, the Irish Free State was formed, consisting of the twenty six counties of Southern Ireland and was later renamed the Republic of Ireland. The six remaining counties in the North remained part of England, continued to be governed by the Crown, and became known as Northern Ireland. Nationalist supporters in the North felt that the South had sold them out in the deal that divided the nation, and the Irish Republican Army continued to have support for complete removal of English rule in Ireland. The history books were clear that, from then on, the battle lines between the Catholic minority and the Protestant ruling class in Northern Ireland were drastically drawn. This division ultimately led to the modern sectarian warfare known as "the Troubles."

The "Troubles" was the general term for the most recent stage of the conflict between the political and socioeconomic factions in Northern Ireland. Many saw the conflict as a battle between the Protestants and Catholics but in actuality it was more like a battle between the haves and have nots. Mick learned that Catholics in Northern Ireland were treated very similar to the way black people in the United States were treated prior to the Civil Rights movement. The Troubles began in the late 60's and early 70's with peaceful demonstrations for Catholic equality, evolved into riots between the two religious groups, and then exploded into a guerilla war between paramilitary groups. The resurgent Irish Republican Army (IRA) and the Ulster Volunteer Force (UVF) basically tried to kill each other through various brutal beatings, assassinations and bombings. The Catholics who were discriminated against on all economic and cultural fonts supported the nationalist IRA. The more affluent Protestants who wanted to continue their more privileged way of life got behind the UVF and similar groups. Much violence and killing ensued. The result was the occupation of Northern Ireland by British forces presumably sent to "keep the peace" as far as Mick could tell. These same British soldiers had occupied Northern Ireland since July 1970 and were still here.

The most tragic event in the history of the conflict occurred on January 30, 1972, when the British Army shot twenty-six unarmed catholic civil rights demonstrators, killing fourteen of them, including six children. The rest of the world eventually came to know this as "Bloody Sunday." Mick remembered the 1980's song "Sunday

Bloody Sunday" by the Irish band U-2. He never realized what the song was actually about or much at all regarding the turmoil in Northern Ireland that had lead up to that terrible day. He'd heard of the "Troubles" before, knew that it was a sectarian war on which the British tried to intervene, but never really gave it much thought. Like most Irish-Americans, he had always been proud of his heritage but now he realized that he had no real concept of what it meant to be Irish, especially if you were an Irish Catholic in Northern Ireland. There was a sadness to this history that most of the world did not know. He felt a wave of guilt fall over him as he recognized that he himself never really took the time to learn a damn thing about his ancestry. Mick sat up straight in his chair as he began to realize for the first time that the history of this torn and battered country was now inextricably part of him and part of Sarah. She was a victim of "the Troubles."

Although the Troubles had been going on for many years, the most recent history books and the daily newspapers indicated there was hope for peace in Northern Ireland. In 1985, the Irish government had been granted a consultant role in its own government. For the past five years there had been discussions between the Irish and British governments about possible complete withdrawal of British troops, and the total return of the government of Northern Ireland to the people of Northern Ireland. Many deals were laid out and all of the attempts failed. One of the largest hurdles was the request that the paramilitary organizations, particularly the IRA, turn over their weapons. Until recently, the IRA had resisted the decommissioning of their weapons in what it considered a war against Britain. Various cease fires on both sides were issued and rescinded, resulting in more bombings, shootings, and death. Almost two years ago, however, the IRA agreed to a cease fire and the nationalistic approach shifted drastically from the direct antagonistic activities of the IRA, to the more reasoned peaceful actions of its political wing, Sinn Féin, which sought to gain Irish freedom through political maneuvering without the use of force.

The last two month's papers were jam packed with news of United States Senator George Mitchell's efforts to broker a deal called "The Belfast Agreement" which could ultimately lead to Irish freedom. The agreement would allow Northern Ireland's government to rule itself and to succeed from the British union and rejoin the Republic of Ireland if and when the majority of the voters in Northern Ireland so chose. Basically, it removed the chains that had been tied around Northern Ireland and allowed it to leave the United Kingdom if it wanted to. Freedom to leave, but with the invitation to stay and enjoy the economic benefits of being part of Britain summed up the agreement. Although the deal would eventually need to be approved by referendum, there was a good possibility that it would be accepted by the people in the North, even though the majority was Protestant and loyalist. Only one of the major political parties, the Democratic Unionist Party, vehemently opposed the plan. As far as Mick could tell, Sinn Féin, the IRA, the loyalist groups, all of the other political parties, the British government, and Senator Mitchell were very close to pulling this off. Mick shook his head in wonder as he realized that he had no idea all this was going on just weeks ago as he and Sarah flitted around the Irish country side like clueless tourists. He

wondered if Sarah, who had a much better sense for current events and politics, had been aware of it all.
Within a matter of weeks, maybe days, Ireland could be free and Mick could be here during one of the most historic moments in the country's long and turbulent history.

Mick leaned back in his chair and starred at the lights in the library ceiling thinking what a price he had paid for this front row seat.

Chapter 6

THE CUSTOMS PIER AT DOCK 16 in Dublin looked fairly empty just as Johnny Herndon, also known as Sean Ryan to the FBI, pulled his rented moving van up to the Harbor Master's office. A quick trip into the building and he picked up his confirmation documents with an obligatory rubber-stamp and not so much as a question from the stiff working at the shipping counter. This was easier than he thought. Little did he know, the FBI and Dublin Police Department had streamlined the process just for him. To help put the finishing touches on the trans-Atlantic sting, Special Agent in Charge Cecil Maxwell enlisted two local police officers to work alongside four FBI agents stationed at the American Embassy in London who were occasionally assigned to his command: agents Storm, Michelson, James, and Roberson. The six had been surveilling the port for the second day when Herndon finally arrived. The long awaited sting operation, set up to capture the recipient of the AK-47 shipment, was officially underway at last.

Herndon was directed to hop back into the truck and follow the blue stripe on the road to lot 9D where he would find his container. A half an hour to load the truck and he would be gone. Simple. The lock on the container was his own. Only he had the key. The Master Lock key jostled on his key chain in the van's ignition as he followed the blue stripe. He didn't know that his original lock had been removed with bolt cutters by U.S. Customs agents just before the container's week long voyage to the Emerald Isle. He didn't know that his precious AK-47's and grenades were being watched at this very moment by four FBI agents and two Dublin police officers. He didn't know the feds had worked quickly with the remains of his Master Lock to fashion a duplicate that could only be worked by his key. And he didn't know the six were ready to pounce on him the second he took possession of the weapons.

Catching Herndon red handed was important since under both Irish and American law, the authorities needed to catch him removing the contraband from the container and physically taking possession of it to implicate him in a crime. His showing up was not enough. He had to physically receive the weapons in order to be held, booked, and eventually prosecuted for foreign arms dealing, terrorism, and whatever else he would eventually be charged with. Holding him for interrogation was tops on the list of things the feds wanted to do to Johnny Herndon. He would be interrogated at length regarding the American source of the weapons. This was the big break for "The Unit" as they finally had someone nailed and they would use this opportunity to catch the bigger fish. Lead agent Barry Storm had strict instructions from Maxwell in the United States to do everything by the book. Herndon was not to escape and was to be taken alive.

Herndon pulled up to lot 9D. Agent Storm, sitting at the base of a cargo crane, watched in silence, then radioed back to the Harbor Master's office, and the dock's heavy security gates were bolted shut. The local police were stationed just inside the gate in case

Herndon attempted to flee. As Herndon came to a stop, Storm radioed Michelson, James, and Roberson, who were stationed behind lots 9C, 9E, and 10D, telling them, "The target is on the move. Stand ready. Maintain radio silence. Move on my command." He would not turn the agents loose until Herndon had his hands on the stash.

Herndon stepped from the truck in jeans and a hooded sweatshirt, pretending to fumble for the right key as he scoped left and right to see if anyone was watching. It was clear. He wondered to himself why the New Republican Brotherhood didn't have more great gear like this when smuggling the guns and grenades was such a piece of cake? Still, he held his breath as he turned the key. Click. The bolt sprung open and he released the air from his lungs. The lock came off easily but he had to struggle with the heavy door bars of the container which only moved with brute force once the lock was removed. The four hundred pound door creaked loudly as he pulled it open and stepped inside to the darkness. After a few seconds, Herndon's pupils adjusted and he stepped behind the ragged love seat, coffee table, dinette set, and other various junk furniture he had bought to fill up the container and hide the crates of weapons. As he surveyed the cargo, he thought that everything appeared to be stacked in a slightly different way. He wrote it off to shifting of cargo during the week long sea voyage. He peeked behind the dining room table and chairs and there they sat – the seventeen crates he had loaded in Brooklyn. Untouched. Perfect. He carried a lamp out of the container to take another look around and spent the next twenty minutes clearing a path wide enough to wheel the crates out on a dolly.

Agent Storm watched patiently as Herndon wheeled out the first crate, and then the second. Storm watched Herndon bend and struggle to get each of crates off the dolly and into the van. The moment of struggle with each crate was the perfect time to strike. As Herndon wheeled out the third crate and bent down to lift one end onto the back bumper of the van, Agent Storm pressed the red button on his walkie and whispered, "Take him. Now!" All four agents converged on Herndon as he bent and lifted one end of the crate. As they ran toward him Herndon heard the gravel crushing under their feet, dropped the crate of weapons, and quickly darted between the huge red containers sitting on lots 10B and 10C. He was headed towards the locals who were securing the perimeter. Storm jumped down from the crane and radioed the Unit telling them to, "Keep contain! Do not lose him!" He could see agents Michelson and James creeping between the containers with their weapons drawn, ready to shoot anything that moved. Suddenly, a bullet ricocheted off the steel near Agent Michelson's head. Both men ducked and spread out. Storm quickly crossed the road between lot rows 9 and 10 and headed in the direction of the gun shot. He caught Agent James out of the corner of his eye and signaled for him to sweep right while Storm swept left.

James nodded then looked at Storm again with a look of horror on his face as he slowly raised his .357 Magnum and pointed it right at Storm. Storm wondered for a second why James would point his gun in Storm's direction. Then he realized – Herndon was behind him. Storm heard Herndon's gun click next to his right ear and felt its cold steel tip press against his temple as Herndon whispered from behind, "Move and you die."

Storm dropped his hands to his sides. Herndon relieved him of his weapon, stuffed it into his belt and wrapped his left arm around Storm's throat, dragging his new hostage out into the middle of the gravel road where everyone could see who now had the upper hand. James kept his weapon pointed at the two men and followed every step. Herndon glared at James with sweat dripping down the sides of his face. James, Michelson, and Roberson, surrounded Herndon. Herndon yelled, "Put down your guns." His voice quivered with fear.

Storm commanded, "Do what he says." They needed Herndon alive, plus Herndon was holding Storm too closely – way too close for one of the agents to take a heroic shot at him with inaccurate hand guns.

"Back down the driveway as far as you can or he dies," the Irishman yelled as he backed away from the agents.

The agents slowly placed their weapons on the ground and backed about a hundred feet back. Herndon was scared. He didn't want to kill anyone but he wasn't about to go to prison. His brother, Matty, had done time in Long Kesh and died on the inside. That was not going to happen to him.

"Stop right there," Herndon yelled and looked over his shoulder to the other end of the road which dead ended into a chain link fence. The other agents knew if they went on the offensive Storm was dead. Herndon looked away from them again; he was looking for something on the other side of fence about eighty feet away. Storm felt Herndon's attention focus elsewhere as he continued to look over his shoulder at the other side of the fence.

A brown Ford Cortina suddenly appeared on the other side of the fence. Herndon forced Storm to the ground until he was flat on his belly. Herndon's emergency back up had finally just arrived. As Storm lay face down in the gravel, unarmed, and the three other agents stood a hundred feet from their guns, Herndon cold cocked Storm, turned his back and started running toward the fence. He could climb the fence and speed away in a little less time than it would take the agents to get to their weapons. It would be close but it was his only chance at escape. Storm rolled over in pain and the gravel flew out from under the agents' shoes as they raced towards their guns.

When Herndon was about thirty feet from the fence, the rear passenger window of the Cortina rolled half way down and the end of a semi-automatic rifle rested gently on the edge of the glass. Herndon was running so fast he never noticed the gun. Herndon's emergency backup didn't quite agree that he could make it over the fence in time. The backup correctly assessed the situation and feared Herndon would be caught alive and forced to tell everything he knew. There was no way Herndon was going to make it. Not with the barbed wire at the top of the fence. The agents would have him in a matter of seconds. Herndon failed to see the razor sharp wire and had failed to take it into account. His compatriots knew he was weak, and he would talk. It was best to dispose of him now.

The first gun shot hit Herndon in the stomach, the second hit him in the face, and the third blew off a piece of his head. His head jolted backwards as he stopped dead in his tracks and dropped slowly to the ground, his knees hitting the blacktop first as his arms hung limply at his side. He balanced on his knees for a split second not quite comprehending what had just happened as his torso crashed to the ground with a thud. The side of his cheek felt cold on the damp asphalt near the fence as his pupils began to widen. Blood dripped from the side of his head across his eyes and upper lip and began to pool underneath his head. Herndon's eyes fixated blankly and stared sideways on the horizon, right at the spot the Cortina had just vacated as he slowly mouthed the words, "Fuck you Fergus." None of the agents heard him.

"Dammit!" yelled Storm as he knelt down and felt no pulse on Herndon's wrist. He walked somberly back to the car to call Maxwell back in New York to let him know that the FBI's best lead in three years had just breathed his last breath through a mouthful of gurgling blood, lying face down in a pile of his own gray matter. Special Agent in Charge Cecil Maxwell would not be happy.

Chapter 7

THE DECISION to take a "wee holiday" as the O'Neils called it was an easy one. Big Tom presented the idea at dinner the night before and Mrs. O'Neil didn't even really ask Mick if he wanted to go. It was assumed.

"Let's try to get on the road by eight o'clock in the morning," she said. "We'll have a quick breakfast and be on our way. Right." Mick didn't recall saying a single word during the entire conversation. Nonetheless, he was about to go on vacation with the family that seemed to have adopted him and had no intention of asking him to leave.

The idea of a vacation appealed to Mick. Although he'd only been to work one day in the past four weeks, he had been working the library six to eight hours a day and he needed some time to relax, rest, and come to grips with the reality of what life was now going to be like without Sarah. He'd been keeping pretty busy, so as not to be alone with his thoughts, but some quiet time in the country just might be the thing he needed.

Mick packed all of his clothes into his duffle bag and walked down stairs, past the living room photographs of Jesus, Pope John Paul II, John F. Kennedy, and the beautiful young Mairead O'Neil, who looked to be about age seven in the photograph. Mick gathered from Big Tom that Mairead died in 1981 in some sort of tragedy; however, Big Tom didn't offer any other information and Mick just didn't have the heart to ask.

"Good morning," said Mick as he sat down to a plate of piping hot scone just pulled from the oven. Mrs. O'Neil bent across the table and set down a huge mug of tea, just the way Mick liked it, and said, "How'd you sleep?"

"Like a baby," Mick said, lying to his host as he slathered the creamy Irish butter onto his first scone. The truth was that, in fact, every night for the past week he had nightmares in which Sarah was alive but which always ended with her dying some horrible death. Sometimes it was the car bomb; sometimes it was something else. On two occasions he had woken up in a cold panicked sweat and thought he heard himself screaming as he awoke. He was not sure if the O'Neils had heard his night terrors and he wasn't about to trouble them with the details concerning something they could do nothing about.

"Good, you needed a good night's sleep," she said. By her response Mick figured she knew.

Mick took a huge gulp of the tea which Mrs. O'Neil prepared with two sugars and almost half a cup of milk. Mick had never been a big tea drinker but ever since becoming the O'Neil's house guest he was quickly becoming addicted to the stuff. The teapot in the O'Neil home was never off the stove. Big Tom and Mrs. O'Neil must have drunk ten or twelve cups each during the day. Mick was up to about five or six a day himself. He would even order tea with his lunch every day when he took a break and headed across the street from the library for some food. He half seriously wondered if the love of tea was somehow genetic and whether it had just been lying dormant in his Irish genes all these years.

Big Tom walked into the house from the front door and said, "We're all loaded up." Tom had apparently already eaten and Mrs. O'Neil was filling a thermos with tea. Mick choked down the rest of his scone as Mrs. O'Neil went back into the kitchen to put away the butter.

"Let's roll," said Mick. "Where are we off to?"

"Killybegs," said Tom with an unexpected excitement in his voice. The trio headed out the door and loaded into Tom's old station wagon. Thankfully, Tom had removed the ladders and painter's tools that usually filled up the back seat and rear hatch area. Tom had offered to take Mick to work with him on one occasion but Mick declined thinking that the big fella was just trying to be nice. Plus, Mick had some money and he knew he would likely be taking the job of someone who really needed the work.

"So, what's in Killybegs?" said Mick.

"My auntie owns a wee campsite there and we can stay for free during the off season. She's a bit slow right now before the schools let out for Easter so it's a good time to visit," said Mrs. O'Neil.

"How far away is the campsite?" asked Mick.

"Oh, I'd say we'll be there in about an hour and a half," replied Mrs. O'Neil. "Maybe sooner the way old lead foot here drives."

Mick and Tom chuckled. It was clear that the O'Neils really loved each other and their love was most evident in the way Big Tom never questioned what his wife asked him to do and in the way they gently teased each other. Yet, there was a sadness between the two. At times, each had the faraway look that only people who have lost a child seem to have. There was some deep down grief that seemed to haunt them both but which also seemed to release when they were around others.

Mick figured this was why they had opened their home to him. He was someone in need of caring, and they were people who longed to take care of someone again.

Within ten minutes, the station wagon had left the Belfast city limits and was headed out on what appeared to be the same highway that Mick and Sarah had taken to the city. The suburbs lasted another fifteen minutes and soon the O'Neil camping expedition was cruising through the rolling Irish country side. After about an hour, they entered a town and passed a sign that said, "YOU ARE NOW ENTERING FREE DERRY." As they passed the sign, Big Tom popped a tape into the car's ancient cassette recorder and the sounds of Irish folk music floated throughout the car from the cheap tinny speakers. The green, white and orange tricolor of the Republic flew here even though this was the North where all Mick had thus far only seen the English Union Jack flown sporadically.

The singer on the car radio sang about playing ball as a boy in a poor town where women worked in a shirt factory, while their unemployed husbands got the children out to school in the morning then walked the docks looking for work. The song went on to say how proud he was of the town that he loved with all his heart. He continued on about how music filled the air of the small town and how he formed a small musical band but eventually left the town behind, fell in love, and got married.

Mick thought about Sarah as he listened to the tune's evocative melody and touching lyrics. A familiar lump began to grow in his throat. He leaned forward in his seat and asked, "Who's this singing?"

"That's Phil Coulter," said Big Tom.

"It's such a beautiful song," said Mick, "What is the town that he's singing about?"

"You're in it," said Mrs. O'Neil, turning and smiling.

"Derry?"

"Yes."

Mick asked about the "FREE DERRY" sign and the O'Neils took turns explaining that this particular area in Derry, "Londonderry" as the loyalists called it, was the one neighborhood in town that was barricaded off by the residents, many of whom were armed IRA members, who dared the British soldiers to try to come in. This was one part of the country "the Brits" would not have. Mick settled back into his seat, closed his eyes and tried to picture the life of the people in the tune.

As they drove on, Phil Coulter crooned with deep sadness about having returned to the town later only to see it devastated by The Troubles.

He spoke of tanks, guns, barbed wire, the installation of an army, and the spirit of the town being damaged but never destroyed. He sang of how the people in the town remembered the past, which can never be changed, and how they now hope and pray for peace and a new future.

"So sad but so beautiful," Mick said to himself. The town gave way to farmland again and Mick stared blankly out the window as the pastures and cows whizzed by. He felt a warm tear fall onto his hand. He didn't know if he was crying for Sarah or for Ireland and the Irish people.

The station wagon was waved through the North-South border crossing by a smiling British soldier. Within thirty minutes the car pulled up to the sign which read, "Morrissey's Caravanning and Camping Grounds." Auntie Mary was weeding the garden out front as they pulled into the drive. The site was a small North Western coastal campground with eight hotel rooms and ten caravans for rent, twenty acres of land for anyone who wanted to pitch a tent for sixteen pounds a night, and a small restaurant which served breakfast and dinner. Auntie Mary Morrissey, a seventy-four year old woman whose husband died from cancer five years ago, was Mrs. O'Neil's favorite aunt. She and her children ran the place and were able to make a decent living when the tourists hit the Donegal area for the summer. The campgrounds sat at the edge of Killybegs, a bustling Irish fishing village with enough tourist attractions and shopping nearby to keep the visitors coming. The camp site was situated on the outskirts of town, right behind the dunes on the beach stretched out before the Atlantic Ocean. Mick was slightly disappointed when he realized they were staying in the house attached to the hotel and not the caravans he saw off in the distance. What sort of camping was done indoors anyway?

After a quick hello and introduction to Auntie Mary, Mick left his bag in the car, kicked off his shoes, and headed down the trail to the beach as the O'Neils headed up to Auntie Mary's house which was attached to the hotel. Surely, the O'Neils were explaining who he was to Auntie Mary. Mick imagined Auntie Mary's face as she sat and listened to the story of how Mick McKenna landed on the O'Neil's front steps.

On his way to the beach, Mick noticed the doors on two un-rented caravans were open. He stepped inside to take a look inside the older aluminum half size camper. He saw two beds, a fold down kitchen table and just enough room in between it all to walk in and out of the door. It was dingy and old, but it was clean. Auntie

Mary had put fresh sheets and heavy wool blankets on the beds, along with what appeared to be brand new pillows. A naked overhead light bulb gave the camper a dim glow. He started to breathe heavy in the close quarters and thanked God that they were not staying in the campers after all with his recent battles against claustrophobia. He stepped out onto the cool sand and bright light and continued on the trail down to the beach.

The sand on this side of the Atlantic was much more coarse than the sand at the Jersey Shore where Mick had vacationed his entire life. The grittiness of the Irish sand felt good between his toes. As Mick stepped between the last two dunes, the waves were crashing against a jetty and shooting high in the air while an eerie morning mist hovered over the ocean. Mick plopped down on the cold sand. He began sucking in the salty cool air with his legs crossed, letting handful after handful of sand slowly fall through his fingers. The sound of gulls overhead and the monotonous crash of the heavy waves falling onto the shoreline put him at ease. After about a half an hour, the sun broke through the gray sky and suddenly the beach grew warmer. The morning mist and haze quickly burned off. The heat felt good on his face and Mick began to relax. He pulled off his sweater and rolled it into a pillow. He laid down flat on his back, looked up at the pale blue sky peeking out from behind an almost black cloud and closed his eyes. His relaxed mind immediately began to wander. He thought about the hugeness of the ocean, the massive size of the Earth, the endlessness of the Universe, and his own insignificance in the scope of it all. He began to think about the meaning of life and then about his own death. Death had previously scared the hell out of him,

but the fear was no longer so ominous.
Now, his thoughts seemed to focus on death as way to be with Sarah again someday. Even though he was angry at God for allowing Sarah to be taken away from him at such a young age, her death oddly seemed to have strengthened his belief in an afterlife.
He often wondered if he was just telling himself that to make himself feel good. Still, he walked to Mass with the O'Neils every Sunday and felt Sarah's presence each time he walked through the doors of Saint Bridget's Church. Such heavy existential thoughts were tiring and before long the repetitive crash of the surf rocked Mick to sleep.

Mick popped up onto his elbows and opened his eyes wide as someone shook his shoulder to wake him. She had moved his shoulder ever so gently but Mick jumped like he had been shot because he was in such a sound sleep. He rubbed his eyes and wondered how long he had been out as he confusingly focused on the long dark brown hair and heavy Aran sweater of a woman, kneeling down next to him.

"Mr. McKenna. Hi. Sorry to startle you, but if you don't wake up now, you're going to float away," the woman said pointing toward the ocean and laughing.

The tide had come in and the waves were crashing and dying about five feet from his toes. Mick, still groggy, pulled his legs back and smiled.

"Thanks," he said, "how do you know my name?"

The next wave was bigger than the last and crashed right on top of Mick's feet, soaking the bottom of the woman's pants and Mick from the waist down. They both let out surprised yells as Mick grabbed his sweater and they ran away from the tide to the higher ground. Mick helped the woman up onto the closest mini-dune.

"I'm Jillian Morrissey," the woman said.

Mick extended his hand to shake, "Do you always walk around waking up strange men?"

"Only when they are in danger of taking an unexpected dip in the Atlantic."

"Thank God for that," Mick said, smiling.

Jillian Morrissey was a typical Irish beauty. Her long dark brown hair was naturally wavy and somewhat unruly as the beach winds blew it back and forth around her beautiful milky white skin and deep blue eyes. She was about five foot four with thick and exotic eye brows. Mick couldn't help but stare. He figured she was about thirty two years old.

"So, you run this place?" asked Mick.

"Well, Mary, my Mum, runs things. I just help her out since my father died," said Jillian.

"I'm sorry to hear about your father," said Mick.

"Oh, don't be sorry, he had a great life." She paused and then said, "We'll all be together again someday." It was as if she had been listening to Mick's thoughts just before he drifted off. He noticed the tiny Celtic cross hanging from a simple chain around her neck.

"I hope you're right about that," he said.

"I am," she said, full of faith, and smiled before she looked away as if she did not want to make him feel uncomfortable. Mick could tell she had already heard his story and really hadn't anticipated talking to him about death two minutes after they had met. But it was too late now.

"It's okay. It's probably good for me to talk about it," Mick offered.

"I'm sorry to hear about your wife," she said heading down the beach to toward the jetty.

"Thank you," Mick said. He followed her down the beach.

"This family's no stranger to the Troubles," said Jillian.

"How so?" Mick asked.

"Mairead, my cousin," said Jillian turning her head so that Mick could not see her eyes mist up.

They walked another fifty yards. Mick didn't say a word.

"The poor wee angel was walking to the store to buy a bottle of milk when she was hit by a rubber bullet?"

Mick listened but Jillian saw the puzzled look on his face.

She explained, "It's a bullet that the Brits shoot into a crowd to make everyone scatter. There was a bunch of teenagers standing on the corner throwing bottles at the soldiers about fifteen years ago and the bastards shot at them. She was just walking by."

"How did something made of rubber kill her?" Mick inquired.

"They're rock hard and weigh about a quarter pound. They're supposed to be aimed at the legs and shot from a long distance during riots. This was just three or four kids throwing glass at a tank. One of the soldiers thought it would be fun to scatter the boys with a shot. The bullet bounced off the curb and ricocheted into Mairead's face. She was in a coma for two days and lost her left eye. They thought she was going to make it at first but the trauma to her head was so massive that her brain swelled until she died of a stroke. She was only eight years old. Her Mum and Dad have never been the same since," said Jillian.

Mick was staggered by the revelation. The O'Neils were victims of the Troubles too. He climbed up the steep black rocks of the jetty and reached down to pull up Jillian. They slowly walked down to the end of the jetty and stood staring out at the turbulent sea. Jillian wiped a tear from the corner of her eye and let out a breath.

Trying to change the subject Mick blurted, "Anything fun to do around here at night?"

"Well, a few of the crowd are heading into the North tonight for a few pints. We'd love for you to come along if you're interested. What do you say?"

"I'm in. Far be it for me to turn down and invitation for a few drinks."

"You sure sound like an O'Neil," she said with a smirk. "Let's plan on it then."

Mick and Jillian walked back up to the house. On the narrow trails that squeezed between the dunes, she walked ahead of Mick. He was surprised that he was paying attention to her body. He even thought about whether they were related and concluded that, even if the McKenna's were related to the O'Neils, the Morrissey's were from Mrs. O'Neil's side of the family, so Jillian and he couldn't even be blood relatives. She was curvy in all the right places. Mick felt guilty as he walked behind her and had a real good chance to see her without her seeing him. He looked away feeling it was inappropriate for him to be attracted to another woman a month after Sarah's death. He never expected to have to deal with the prospect of physical attraction so soon. He quickly shook the thoughts from his head. None of it mattered anyway. He was still married to Sarah.

Up at the house Auntie Mary zipped around the kitchen making finger sandwiches of turkey and ham, and, of course, tea. She moved with the speed of a thirty year-old woman and aside from her wrinkled face and bony hands no one would ever suspect she was in her seventies. She refused any help from her guests. The house was an old

Tudor structure that reminded Mick of the many B&B's where he and Sarah had stayed. Jillian had some paperwork to do so she just grabbed half a sandwich and kissed Big Tom and Mrs. O'Neil as she excused herself into the back room which housed a makeshift office. They all sat around the kitchen table for lunch.

"Some of the cousins are coming around tonight for a bit of a party Mick, it should be a good time," said Auntie Mary."

Mick was caught off guard and stammered, "Well, actually, Jillian just invited me to go out with her and some friends tonight. I don't know what time we are leaving but I would love to meet everyone."

"Oh, I'm sure some of the cousins are in on the trip so I'm sure you're not leaving 'til they get here," Aunt Mary said, letting him off the hook.

"Sounds good to me," said Mick.

Mick spent the rest of the day walking down to the little village near the docks and taking in the local shops and pubs. As he began to walk down a country road into the town he was surprised when a car pulled up and the driver said, "Going into town? Hop in, I'll give you a lift." The driver was a red headed boy around seventeen named Seamus. He knew the Morrisseys, Jillian, and even the O'Neils. He provided the ride like it was the most natural thing in the world to offer a stranger a ride into town. Apparently, it was done here every day. After the five minute drive, Mick thanked him and stood in amazement as Seamus pulled away, thinking how he would never have gotten into a stranger's car in America and how only the most daring of sorts would ever pick up a hitchhiker back in the States. Things were simpler here.

Everyone he met was friendly and more than happy to answer any questions he had about the town and locals. The Irish accents were much thicker here, out in the country, and he had a hard time understanding everyone.

Mick sat on a bench for about two hours watching various fishermen pull into the docks and unload their catches. After the first hour he understood the routine and began to watch the people. He was fascinated by the interaction of the men who worked the nets and cranes. He imagined how he would have fared making a living on his daily hauls from a fishing boat. Mick didn't know a great deal about fishing but it seemed like an honorable way to make a living. The work was hard but the men of the sea laughed and joked while they worked and moved at their own pace. The docks were alive with action, but there was no sense of urgency in anything the fishermen did. Yet, it all moved like clockwork.

Theirs was a simple yet joyful life and Mick, after all that had happened, longed for something like it.

Earlier, Mick had walked by a man building a brick pier on his way into town and he walked by the same man on the way back to the campsite. The man had only laid another twenty or so brick in the two hours since Mick initially passed and was sitting on his tool box eating a bun, drinking his cup of tea, and chatting with his laborer as Mick walked by and said hello. Both men gave a smile and continued their conversation without a care in the world. Everything seemed to move much slower here.

Chapter 8

ROBBIE GLEASON HONKED THE HORN a second time, frustrated that Jillian didn't immediately produce herself on the first honk. He was too lazy and ignorant to get out of his car and go up to the house like a decent boyfriend would. Inside the house, Jillian greeted and kissed all of the Aunts and Uncles and cousins and half cousins who had arrived to visit with the O'Neils who were only in town a couple of times a year. She briefly introduced Mick to everyone and they promised they would be back from the pub to enjoy the end of the party. Robbie honked again. As Mick and Jillian headed out the front door, two of the cousins said they might catch up with them later at the pub.

"Fuck," whispered Robbie when he saw that Jillian was with a friend. He hated most of her friends but tolerated them. Jillian's friends never understood why she was with such a loser but she always told them there was a softer, kinder side of Robbie that he only let her see.

Jillian jumped in the front seat and Mick awkwardly slinked into the seat behind her. "This is Mick McKenna here on holiday from America. He's staying with my auntie in Belfast and they're here for a couple of days," said Jillian, "Mick, this is Robbie."

"Hello," said Robbie without even turning his head as he pulled from the curb. He was obviously not a friendly type and Mick thought he was quite rude.

"Nice to meet you Robbie," Mick said as Jillian turned and smiled at him.

"Where to?" asked Robbie.

"Katie and Bridget are meeting us a Castle Ray."

"Great," said Robbie with a sarcastic sneer. He knew they were going to be heading to some club across the border but he was hoping none of Jillian's friends were going to join them.

"Don't start your shit," Jillian said. Mick was surprised by her tone but proud of her for giving it to Robbie like that. Robbie was silent for the rest of the thirty-minute trek back into the North.

Castle Ray was a dance club inside a renovated castle in a small town just over the border between Northern Ireland and the Republic of Ireland. Tonight the road gate was down and

Robbie stopped at the guard shack. A soldier asked to see his license and looked in the window at Mick and Jillian. Without saying anything he handed back the license and went inside the kiosk. The gate lifted and Robbie drove through.

Castle Ray was hopping. Mick was shocked to see a New York style dance club in the middle of a tiny European town. "Frankie Goes to Hollywood – Relax, Don't Do It" was blasting out of the massive speakers scattered all over the hall while strobe lights bounced and flickered off the sweaty bodies gyrating all over the dance floor. Jillian saw Katie and Bridget out on the floor. "Oh, I love this song," she said, leaving Mick and Robbie standing at a small circular table near the bar. Robbie had the personality of a wet blanket so Mick asked, "What can I get you to drink?" just to get away from him.

Robbie said, "Smithwick's" and Mick headed to the bar, glad to be away from Robbie the dud. The bar was packed seven deep with people clamoring for a drink. This was apparently the only New York style dance club within a hundred miles.

As Mick waited, he watched Jillian on the dance floor. She had a lot of rhythm and he couldn't help but wonder what she was like in bed. She was very sexual. Maybe it was the sweat, maybe it was the way she was moving, or maybe it was just her amazing smile and gorgeous hair. It could have been her flat belly or the naked small of her back that showed when her short shirt started to ride up when she moved. Whatever it was she was sexy. He wondered if he would ever have sex with another woman and whether Sarah would have wanted him to. He couldn't believe he was thinking about sex with another woman while his wife's still warm corpse lay rotting in a box back in Pennsylvania. He started to feel guilty and questioned whether the sexual feelings and need for physical contact were somehow related to the grief he had not yet dealt with. He was still alive and surely he would have sex again. Someday. With someone. But now was just too soon.

When Mick returned with the drinks, Robbie was off in the corner talking to a guy with short spiky hair, motioning in Mick's direction. He was obviously talking about Mick. Robbie had a drink in his hand already so Mick hung near table. The three girls came by soon. Jillian's two friends were very friendly. Katie worked at the Irish version of the DMV and Bridget worked with children in foster care. Mick chatted with the girls as Jillian went over to speak with Robbie. There was talk about heading to a pub down the road which was guaranteed to be less crowded. Jillian and Robbie were certainly fighting about it and Mick overheard Robbie say, "Go. I don't give a fuck! But be back here by eleven or you can find another way home."

Jillian walked back over to the table and explained, "Robbie isn't really that interested but he wants us to go ahead and have good time." She smiled and everyone laughed because they all knew his real position.

Findlay's was a traditional Irish pub with cozy little booths and people sitting at table after table drinking their pints, laughing and enjoying each other's company. It struck Mick that this was the real center of socialization in the poor country. Most people didn't have money to belong to country clubs and involve themselves in high society activities. This was where people came to meet and greet, where everyone knew everyone else, and learned about what was going on in the community. It was simple and honest and real and Mick realized that he didn't have something similar to this in the states.

A juke box played a vast array of music. First, Tina Turner's "What's Love Got To Do With It" then an Irish folk song, then Duran Duran's "Rio." The music in the jukebox was about a decade behind the times but it was good. Katie and Bridget were on the prowl for men and went to the back room to shoot darts with a few guys they knew from Derry.

Jillian and Mick sat in a comfortable booth in the corner and before lone they were talking like old friends. Jillian had three pints to Mick's two and Mick was starting to feel the effect of the alcohol. She seemed untouched. She was a smart girl and she explained the Troubles to him in great detail. She explained that, "In Belfast there is literally and physically a wall built between the Protestant and Catholic neighborhoods. Everyone has basically picked a side."

"The O'Neils and the Morrisseys have always been Nationalists. You know, Republicans." This made sense to Mick since he knew they supported the Irish Republican Army.

She explained, "My aunt and uncle live in a nationalist neighborhood. Ever since you have been here you've been traveling in nationalist circles. You just don't know it."

"How can I see the other side – the Loyalist, the Protestant perspective?" Mick asked.

"I really don't know. All these years, I really don't know what Protestants are like. You see, in the North, you are born one way and most of us learn to hate the other side. Right or wrong. That's just what happens. Most people never give it a second thought. It's all they know," she said.

"Do you hate them?" Mick pried.

"No. I understand that they are all born into this situation just like I have been. Who chooses to be in a war zone? I have a few casual Protestant friends but I have no real perspective on the Loyalist view," said Jillian.

"It's like the blacks and whites in America," Mick said, "There is no real overt racism going on any more but the two cultures as a general rule are still very, very different and rarely mix."

Jillian suspected that the Protestants saw the Troubles the same way on their side. Everybody just followed along like sheep. Especially the older people who lived through the more turbulent times.

"The peace on the horizon is changing things though," she said, "It's relatively clear now that both sides, Nationalist and Loyalist, Catholic and Protestant, rich and poor, are all just sick of the violence. Although it will probably take a hell of a long time to get over the divisions and wounds each side has caused the other, most everyone supports the peace, *in principle*. The violence simply has to end now, even if the underlying distrust of the other side doesn't go away for a while. A lot of the hatred has already gone but some stills lingers in the memories of most families."

Mick was impressed by her ability to boil the whole situation down and explain it to him in such a reasonable well thought out way. She was beautiful and also clearly intelligent.

Bridget and Katie stopped by to say they were going to stay and play some snooker with the boys and Jillian gave them a wink and said, "God luck to you."

"Come on Mick, we better head back before Lord Muck leaves us here to walk home," she said. Mick guzzled the end of his pint.

The night was cool and they walked briskly down the deserted street. They walked down the sidewalk side by side in silence. Outside a burned out building on the other side of the road, a group of young punk rockers smashed a bottle against the wall and yelled across the street, "Fuck the Pope, you fenian bastards!"

"Fuck the Queen you wee asshole!" yelled Jillian. Maybe she was feeling the beer after all thought Mick. Or maybe she was just crazy.

Jillian didn't seem scared when the gang rushed across the street and surrounded her and Mick.

"Why don't you grow up you losers?" she said calmly.

The one with no jacket wearing a Johnny Rotten tee shirt said, "Who's the loser, baby?"

Jillian just stared at him. The punk started to reach toward her to touch her hair and Mick, without saying a word, elbowed him in the solar plexus, right into Johnny Rotten's nose to be exact, and twisted the punk's arm behind his back and said, "Here's the part where you get lost," throwing him toward the street.

"Eat shit," came the battle cry from Johnny Rotten's partner as he brought the beer bottle down across Mick's eyebrow. Mick stumbled toward the wall and the gang scattered. They laughed as they ran and yelled back, "How'd you like that asshole?"

The bottle smashed mostly on Mick's arm as he reacted to protect himself but he had a small but deep gash inside his eyebrow where the bottom of the bottle had caught him. He was dazed from the rush of excitement and sat down on the front step of the red brick building. Jillian said, "Oh, that looks nasty. Let me have a look."

She pulled a handkerchief from her purse and leaned in towards him to dab the blood from his head. Her hand was soft as it held Mick's face. She was so close he could smell the fresh scent of the soap on her skin, wafting in the small space between them. For a moment, their eyes met. In an instant they were each caught up in their attraction for one another and the easy feeling of alcohol. If either one leaned forward to make the first move, there would be a kiss, and possibly more. Mick broke the stare, pulled the handkerchief from her hand, pushed it into his cut, and quickly stood all in one motion.

"Well, Robbie's waiting," he said.

"Right," said Jillian, feeling slightly embarrassed and awkward.

The rest of the walk back to Castle Ray was quiet. They both knew what had almost happened. They knew it would have been wrong and that they had done the right thing by pulling back. Still, there was a guilt that hung in the air between them that came from even considering the kiss and what it would have lead to. Jillian wondered what kind of woman would sleep with a man whose wife had just died. Mick wondered what kind of man would have so little respect for his dead wife such that he would even entertain such an idea. Maybe in another place in another time it might be alright. Mick, knowing Jillian was feeling exactly what he was feeling broke the silence and said, "Still friends?"

"Of course," said Jillian.

Robbie was leaning against his car looking down at his watch as they reached the Castle Ray parking lot.

Robbie was much more pleasant on the car ride home. Maybe the liquor had mellowed him or maybe he was just happy to have Jillian back. He seemed a little buzzed but okay to drive. After a while, the dialogue just died and the three cruised along through the pitch dark night in silence.

As the car rounded a bend about a hundred yards before the border gate, the headlights shone on a British soldier standing in the middle of the road pointing an M-16 at the car's windshield as it approached. Jillian turned to look at Mick and smiled as if to say it was alright. Another much taller soldier with another weapon stepped into the light and waved the car to a stop. The soldier motioned with his M-16 for Robbie to pull over to the side of the road. Robbie slowly complied and stopped the vehicle a few feet from the men. Both British soldiers crept closer to the car with their weapons ready to shoot. Mick stared at them through his window.

"Shut the motor off. Everyone, hands out the window. Now!" the tall one ordered.

Robbie turned off the motor and stuck the keys in his pocket. They all rolled down their windows and felt the cold air rush past their hands and fill the car, as the armed men looked on intently.

A second later, five more soldiers bounced from a jeep that sat off the side of the road, hidden by the night. The added soldiers surrounded the car. Then, in succession, Robbie and Jillian were each violently pulled from their seats and thrown up against the car. After seeing Robbie and Jillian taken, Mick sat, agitated, anxiously waiting for his turn to be yanked from the vehicle.

All in one motion, the soldier pulled Mick out and up onto his feet, turned him towards the gunmen, and shoved him forward. Grabbing him crisply by the neck, the man then pushed Mick hard, face down onto the hood of the car, where he joined Robbie and Jillian. Another soldier grabbed his hands and put them behind his head. Soldiers pinned each of their heads down onto the hood. Mick felt the heat from the car hood on his face as he looked across the metal and stared into Jillian's eyes which were partly obscured by the pressing of the soldier's gloved hand. Two other soldiers then thoroughly searched the inside of the car.

"Nothing here," one said.

"Open the boot," yelled the tall one.

"I need the key, the latch won't work."

"Where's the key?"

"It's in my pocket," said Robbie.

The shorter soldier whipped Robbie around and twisted him in such a way as Robbie's ribs scraped against the hood ornament.

"What the fuck!" yelled Robbie.

Suddenly, the tall one grabbed Robbie by the hair, pulled him up straight, and viciously jammed the point of the M-16 in Robbie's mouth as Mick and Jillian watched with their cheeks still pressed to the cooling car hood.

"Don't give us any of your Irish shit or I'll blow your fucking head off!" he barked.

Robbie's eyes bulged out of this head as he stood on his tip toes, attempting to make himself taller so the tip of the gun wouldn't jab into the back of his throat. Mick stared sideways across the car as Jillian's tears dripped down the hood and onto the bumper. A soldier pulled the key from Robbie's coat pocket and headed for the back of the vehicle.

"Nobody inside," came the reply a few seconds later. Apparently, they were looking for someone.

"Alright, move on," the tall one screamed as he pulled the weapon from Robbie's mouth and the grips on Jillian and Mick were simultaneously released. The soldiers glanced at each other and snickered as the stepped away.

Jillian and Mick, slowly peeled themselves off of the car. Robbie was shaking and Mick saw the tears strolling down his cheeks as he got behind the wheel again. Mick exhaled loudly as he crawled into the back seat again.

"Safe home," said the tall one as he bent down and peered into the passenger side with an evil grin, just as Jillian sat. Each of the three quietly closed their door as the soldiers disappeared into the darkness just off the side of the road.

They drove the last hundred yards of Northern Ireland in greater silence and were waived through the checkpoint by a soldier who acted like he had no idea what had just happened. They didn't speak until they were well into the Free State.

"Robbie, are you alright?" whispered Jillian as she leaned over the seat and started rubbing his back as he drove.

"Yes. Do you believe that fucking bastard?" he replied.

"What the hell was that all about?" asked Mick.

"They were obviously looking for someone trying to get out of the North," said Robbie.

"Who?" said Mick.

"Probably somebody in the fucking RA?" answered Robbie, too loudly.

"The RA?" asked Mick, perplexed.

"The IRA," responded Robbie, annoyed that Mick didn't know the colloquialism.

"But I thought there was a cease fire," said Mick.

"There is, but there are a couple of groups of people that have broken off from the RA who are not going to just let things go," explained Robbie, abruptly.

"What do you mean?" asked Mick.

Jillian interjected, "Some within the IRA don't want anything to do with this peace agreement. They have broken off into two or three of their own groups and denounced the IRA's involvement in the peace talks."

"Who are they?" asked Mick.

"Nobody really knows but the IRA has denounced them and has said that violence by these splinter groups is not sanctioned by the IRA," said Jillian.

"What do they call themselves?" asked Mick.

Robbie replied by yelling, "There's one group called the New Republican Brotherhood and another is called the Real IRA. I hope one of them puts a bullet through that tall fucker's head."

"Robbie, stop. You don't mean that," insisted Jillian.

"Don't tell me what the fuck I mean. You weren't the one chewing on an M-16 back there. I could've been fucking killed," snapped Robbie.

"You know they were just trying to scare us," she said.

"Bullocks!" said Robbie turning his head to face Jillian.

Robbie was very upset and the conversation stopped until they reached the campsite driveway.

"Look," said Jillian to Robbie and to Mick, "it's been one hell of a night, just let's not say anything about this to my Mum or anyone back at the house. It's the last thing they all need to hear."

"No problem," said Mick. Robbie didn't answer. He knew he wasn't coming in.

The Morrissey's were in full party mode as Robbie, Jillian and Mick pulled up to the house. Jillian asked Robbie to come inside "just for a wee minute," but he said, "Not tonight. I'll call you."

Robbie's tires squealed as he turned and sped back down the long driveway and disappeared into the night.

Any news of the night's events could wait until the morning. There was no need to put a damper on the party. Jillian and Mick walked up to the house in half shock prepared to put on a happy face.

Chapter 9

THE SMOKE WAS THICK and the voices were wild and loud as Mick and Jillian entered the party. The aunts and uncles and cousins were all sitting in the living room and dining room in several different conversations. Jillian and Mick went into the kitchen to grab a beer. Big Tom and Mrs. O'Neil were deep in conversation with Uncle Silas. They asked how the night was and Mick and Jillian lied, saying it was uneventful and that they had a good time. *Uneventful?* thought Mick.

Never was there a bigger white lie. He hadn't been in a fight in ten years and never saw a guy forced to eat an M-16. It had been an interesting night to say the least.

They went into the living room. Mick noticed a heavyset man in his early forties, with a head of unmanageable curly hair sitting in the corner with an acoustic guitar.

"Come on, Dodger, give us another wee tune," someone yelled from the crowd. Dodger took a swig of what appeared to be the end of a pint of straight whiskey and took a deep drag of his Woodbine cigarette.

"Here's one for the Provies," he said and began to strum. Mick could not make out the words too well and he asked Jillian, "Who are the Provies?"

"It's an IRA song," she replied.

"Oh, those Provies," said Mick with a grin.

The song was about Bobby Sands, the Irish hunger striker and political prisoner who starved himself to death in Long Kesh prison in 1981. Sands and others went on the hunger strike to call the world's attention to the cause for Irish freedom and Margaret Thatcher's government's refusal to afford them the status of political prisoners. Sands and ten other prisoners were allowed to starve themselves to death before the English government gave in. Mick had read about Bobby Sands and the men who died in Long Kesh. The song was powerful. Dodger had a booming voice at times and could carry as sweet melodic tune as well.

Mick sat silent for a while drinking in this nationalist scene and wondering if he supported the cause of the IRA. He was well on his way to drunk now, and in the wake of what had just happened out on the road, his emotions were running high, allowing him to drift easily to the side of the nationalist cause. He wondered whether the English government ever would have considered the peace plan currently in the works had Bobby Sands, Francis Hughes, Raymond McCreesh, Patsy O'Hara, Joe McDonnell, Martin Hurson, Kevin Lynch, Kieran Doherty, Thomas McElwee, and Michael Devine not given up their lives for the sole purpose of showing the rest of the world the brutality and heartlessness of the English government. Mick got chills as he thought about the courage and bravery of these patriots who made the ultimate sacrifice and envisioned how their Mothers and Fathers had looked on powerlessly, unable to help or stop their young but staunch Republican sons from their heading to what should have been an unnecessary fate. He knew for sure that without the threat of the IRA's military attack on the English status quo, the government would continue to ride rough shod over Northern Ireland's six counties, exploiting and plundering the land, unchecked and unfettered for another 800 years. The IRA wasn't always right, or good, or moral, but someone had to stand up, even if the fight wasn't perfect, Mick reasoned. The IRA was an organization filled with people, good and bad, just like any other collection of men and women. From what he had read, the IRA made a lot of mistakes and innocent people were killed. But when viewed as a war, the killing of innocents seemed inevitable. Mick struggled to find a difference between the American revolutionaries and the young men of the IRA who each fought their own war against the imposition of British Rule. It was clear to Mick that without the threat of the IRA, the English government would never leave. Mick thought about all of the free countries and true democracies in the world and recognized that everyone he could think of had struggled against an invader or force like English Imperialism at one time or another before ultimately becoming free. For the first time in his life, Mick realized that freedom was virtually impossible in this so-called civilized world without the threat of force. The IRA served its purpose and it had served it well.

Dodger next began to sing a song that that simply blew Mick away. He played a simple rhythm and sang about the fields of a town called Athenrye. The song was about a lonely young woman, standing outside a prison wall calling to her husband who had been arrested for stealing corn from the British government so that his starving children could live through the night. Dodger also sang about the prison ship that waited in the bay to take the man to a prison colony in Australia and how he and his wife had at one time watched a bird fly free.

A lump grew in Mick's throat and his chest tightened as he looked around the room and saw the passion with which everyone in the room listened to the song. He wasn't the only one about to cry. Although it was obvious that mostly everyone in the room knew the song well since they all sang along during the chorus, every single person in the room was touched by a tremendous love for their country and an amazing desire to see it free someday. From eighty-eight year-old Aggie to twelve year-old Sean Paul, they all had a bond that was born of oppression and hope that someday their people and their land would be free. Mick was inspired by the simple love of country and he secretly wished inside that he had been born in Ireland. Maybe then his life would have been different and Sarah would not be dead. Then again, he might never have met her.

The "sing song," as it was called, went on for a few more hours with other singers joining in and the singing voices becoming louder and more slurred. There were IRA songs sung, poems recited, "party pieces" performed, and jokes told. Mick was pretty drunk by the time the party finally broke up at 2:00 in the morning. Auntie Mary had gone to bed hours earlier and Jillian put Big Tom to bed at midnight and retired herself. Big Tom was so drunk he could hardly stand but had obviously enjoyed his night.

After all the guests had gone, most of them in taxis that Mick called with Jillian's directions, Mick poked his head into the kitchen and saw that the only person still awake was Mrs. O'Neil.

"Mick, come in here love," she slurred.

Mick walked into the kitchen. Her eyes were droopy and her head hung low to one side as she sat in front of a clear glass whiskey jug that had no label. She looked upon him for a second and then managed a huge smile.

"Sit down and have a wee drink with me," she asked.

Mick pulled up a chair and sat down. He was surprised to see her in this condition but was actually glad to see that she was relaxing and having a good time.

"Sure," said Mick.

Mrs. O'Neil poured Mick a double shot and one for herself. The bottle hit the table with a thud when she set it down.

"Here's to Sarah," she said raising her arm high. Mick was taken aback. She had never mentioned Sarah to him since the day he showed up at her door. It seemed like an unwritten rule that they were not going to talk about her death and Mick's reason for being there. Even in Irish-American families,

Mick knew it was common to avoid talking about major problems. Anyway, he hadn't wanted to talk about it.

Mick could not speak and suddenly his grief started to rush over him once more. He simply raised his glass and clinked it to Mrs. O'Neil's. He guzzled the shot not expecting it to taste any worse than a shot of whiskey or rum. The fire in his throat was immediate. If he had spit it out near a candle he would have expected to have seen an immediate shooting flame ten foot long.

"Holy shit!" he yelled and blew air out of his cheeks over and over again trying to cool his mouth. "What the hell was that?"

"Poitín," Mrs. O'Neil said with a slightly sinister laugh.

"Yeah, but what the hell is it?" reiterated Mick.

"I think you call it *moonshine* in America," Mrs. O'Neil replied.

"Well, that will clean you out," said Mick.

"Sure enough," she said.

She began to pour another round, and Mick said, "That's enough for me, no thanks."

"Oh, just one more Mick. You were doing so well," she pleaded with her eyes.

"Okay, just one," Mick gave in.

She poured what appeared to be triples this time and they clinked their glasses once again.

"To Mairead," Mick said, thinking if she could toast his dead wife, he could bring up her dead daughter. Mrs. O'Neil screwed up her nose and gave him an odd look as if she could not believe he had the balls to bring out the girl's name. Then her face relaxed and she smiled with an appreciative look as if she just realized Mick was perfectly with his rights to bring it up. By the look on her face,

Mick half expected her to say "Touché!"

Instead, she raised her glass and said firmly, "Right – to Mairead. God bless her soul."

Mick smiled and Mrs. O'Neil was touched. Mick's mouth was on fire and he couldn't wait to get upstairs to drain a few glasses of ice cold water.

"Well, I'm going to turn in," he said and without thinking he leaned down and kissed Mrs. O'Neil on the cheek and said, "Good night." Mrs. O'Neil was surprised but pleased by the kiss. She too recognized that they both shared the loss of someone they loved dearly.

"Good night Mick," she said.

Mick gave Mrs. O'Neil one last look as he turned to walk out of the kitchen and saw her wipe a tear from the corner of her eye.

The acid from the vomit burned the back of the throat and crested the back of the tongue and began to leak into Mick's mouth a split second before he shot straight up in the bed. He prayed to God not to let him puke as he ran down the hallway and saw the day's breakfast, lunch and dinner violently eject into the sink. It would have been better to throw up in the toilet but he could only make to the sink. Now he would have to scoop it by hand into the bowl, which was enough to make him want to vomit again. The smell of Poitín was cutting his eyes as he glanced down at his watch. It was almost 4:00 AM and he had only slept for a couple of hours. Suddenly, as he was scooping his now putrid former stomach contents from the sink to the toilet, he heard voices down stairs. He cleaned up his mess and crept to the top of the stairs. All the lights were off. If it was a burglar Mick wanted to have the element of surprise. He felt the aftertaste of vomit mixed with the saliva trickle down the little valley in the middle of his tongue as he peeked his head further down the stairs. In the living room, he heard a woman's voice say, "When your father comes home we will talk about it."

Mick's eyes were still adjusting and he smelled the scent of secondhand smoke before he saw the glow of the cigarette tip moving up and down in the darkness. The voice sounded like Mrs. O'Neil but she didn't smoke as far as Mick knew. Then again, Jillian had told him that a lot of the Irish smoked just when they were "on their holidays."

"Mairead, please don't act like that. We'll discuss it later. There are a hundred reasons why we can't have a puppy in the house. First of all, we don't have the space and it wouldn't be fair to the wee thing to keep it cooped up all day," she said.

There was a pause.

"Yes, I know what the Mallorys do. But we're not the Mallorys are we?" said the woman's voice.

There was another longer pause.

The woman went on, "I know you think you will take care of it and walk it and clean up after it, but that's not all that needs to be considered."

Was there someone talking to someone else at 4:00 in the morning on the phone about a dog? Mick's eyes adjusted to the dark and he peeked down the stairs again. It was weak but he could see a faint silhouette but could not make out the face.

There was another long pause and Mick heard, "Mairead, if you continue to pester me about it I will not speak to your father about it at all." It *was* Mrs. O'Neil. Mick then suddenly realized she was having a conversation with her dead daughter. He laid down at the top of the steps and listened.

"Don't cry darling. Come here," Mick heard her say.

He began to feel guilty for listening to someone else's disturbed private psychosis. As he crept back to his room he heard Mrs. O'Neil whisper, "Now, now. That's right. Let it out. It's okay. I take back what I said. I'll talk to you father about it. It's okay sweetheart. Give me a kiss. I'm sorry I said that. I'm sorry honey. So sorry. Please forgive me. I'm sorry. Oh, my Mairead, Oh, my Mairead, Oh, my sweet darling Mairead… I'm sorry…..I'm sorry… I'm sorry… I'm sorry."

Then, Mrs. O'Neil stopped talking and started to sob intermittently as Mick quietly crept back to his room.

Chapter 10

MICK'S PROTRUDING EYEBROW sat out about two inches and got in the way as he rolled over in the bed. He opened his eyes and reached up to feel the bulbous flesh. It was very sore and much more visible than the night before when the cut had gone unnoticed due to the drunkenness of those at the party and thickness of his eyebrows. It had swollen severely in the night. The pain reminded him of the soreness he last felt many years ago. Mick had always been able to hold his own. As a boy, he got into the normal amount of scrapes and fights. Although he was relatively passive, he never backed down from a fight. His Dad always told him never to start a fight but never walk away. In high school he had been the 198 pound state wrestling champion and went to Michigan State on a sports scholarship. He had a reputation in high school as a quiet guy who everyone knew not to mess with. His reputation was largely attributable to one huge fight he got in during his freshman year at Cardinal McNamara High School in Philadelphia. One spring night, Mick and a few of his buddies went to a dance at a rival Catholic school, Father Connor High. Connor was an all-boys school but the dances were always attended by the most beautiful girls in Northeast Philadelphia. So, of course, the boys from all the surrounding Catholic schools flocked there. Mick and three of his best friends had slammed a few beers in the alley before the dance just to get loose. Two beers each. Not even enough to get drunk. This was a Catholic school and only students from other Catholic schools could attend. The massive crowd lined up down the street and around the corner to show their ID's to get in. The crowd was particularly thick that night. It was the type of crowd in which one literally had to squeeze between people just to walk. Five minutes after the boys from McNamara arrived, Mick squeezed through the crowd towards the men's room and one of the local Connor boys tried to cop a feel while sliding past a pretty blonde girl that had been minding her own business. The girl tried to push the idiot away but the Connor boy grabbed her by the wrist and twisted her arm behind her back, pulling her into him as he stood there laughing his gap toothed laugh, saying "Come on, give me a kiss baby." His free hand was traveling all over the girl's body as she tried to twist from his grip in pain and terror. Mick had seen enough and pushed himself in between the two and the Connor boy released his grip. Mick said, "Just let her go man." The Connor boy put his palm on Mick's shoulder and shoved him hard.

Mick said, "Who the fuck do you think you're pushing?" even though he was a little scared because he was a long way from the protection of his own neighborhood. There were hundreds of Connor boys at this dance and the schools hated each other, mostly due to their football rivalry. Mick would learn later that this was the starting nose guard on the Connor varsity team.

The nose guard got right in Mick's face. He looked down at Mick who was about a foot shorter. Nose guard was a senior and Mick was a freshman.

"You got a problem little man?" the nose guard asked.

"Yeah, I got a problem," Mick retorted.

"Well, do something about it," the bigger man replied.

Mick just stared hard as his buddies pulled him back. "Later," said Bobby McDaid," we just got here." The Connor boys were pulling their man back too. Nobody wanted to get kicked out when the night was so young. The nose guard said, "We'll see you punks for an ass beating at the 54 stop after the dance." Everybody at Connor knew that all the kids at McNamara would take the bus up to Connor from the lower Northeast.

"See you then asshole," said Mick.

The dance was a good time. There were separate bands playing in both the cafeteria and the gym. Mick and his friends talked to a lot of girls. Jimmy Harrington even claimed to have gotten a girl's number.

Just before the dance was over, the Connor boys and the McNamara boys crossed each other's paths once again in the far corner of the gym. The dance had gone on in full force for about three hours and there was only about 15 minutes left. The band was doing an encore as Mick and the nose guard glared at each other. Mick would have preferred to handle things outside. In fact, he was hoping that the two crews wouldn't even run into each other again. It was suddenly clear that there would be no waiting for the bus stop. Mick was hoping that he and his three guys would square off against the lineman and his three friends. However, as Mick and the bigger man continued to stare at each other Mick's friends stepped back as did the other Connor boys. It would be a one on one. A circle started to form.

Mick pulled off his blazer and took off his knit tie. Nose guard watched him closely. Mick was psyching himself up as he rolled up his sleeves, careful not to blink and get caught by the first punch. "Hit me," Mick said. The nose guard looked confused.

"Hit me, asshole." The nose guard looked side to side like he didn't know what to do. Mick was about ten feet away and every time he said "hit me" he felt more and more adrenaline pump through his body. The nose guard had him by about eighty pounds. He was just too big. The only way Mick was going to win this fight was to get hit first and then just explode with rage. But this stupid oaf just grinned at him as Mick said, "Hit me you fucking idiot." The nose guard looked at Mick without fear. Suddenly Mick ran at him, taking about three steps while he threw a roundhouse punch, which landed in the middle of the huge boy's face. Mick stood in shock when the nose guard didn't go down. Mick had hit him with everything he had. *Oh shit*, Mick thought as the two grappled and Mick somehow got up on his feet and put the nose guard in a headlock.

While he had him in the headlock, Mick hammered away on his face. Both boys were wearing dress shoes and sawdust had been sprinkled over the gymnasium floor to protect the finish. It wasn't exactly the type of surface one would hope for when fighting a giant in a pair of wingtips. The two stumbled over near the wooden bleachers, which had been stacked up flat against the wall except for the bottom row which had been left out so the students could sit. Without notice, the nose guard grabbed the back of Mick's head and slammed it into the side of the stacked, hardwood bleachers. The skin above Mick's left eye opened like a flood gate and blood poured down his face into his eyes. He could barely see but when he noticed the blood he went nuts. The big man was not letting go as he continued to slam Mick's head into the wall. Mick realized this fight needed to be over and it needed to be over now. Without thinking, he reached down into his headlock and shoved his index and middle fingers into the other man's nose, right up to the second knuckle, picked up his larger opponent by his nostrils and nasal cavity and slammed the back of his head on the wooden edge of the bottom bleacher step. The fight was over.

The Connor boys rushed to pick up their man from the floor and, since they knew the place, were able to get him out of the school before the priests arrived to break things up. Mick's once bright white shirt was drenched in his own blood as his boys stood by looking at him in amazement. "Wait for me," he said, knowing that there was no way he would be able to escape. He had just kicked the living shit out of a guy twice his size and lived to tell about it and he felt good for a split second until one of the Father Connor priests grabbed Mick's arm and started pulling him through the crowd towards one of the offices. He knew they would call his father and he would be in deep trouble. At least a dozen high school girls screamed in horror as they looked at Mick's face and shirt which were almost completely covered with blood. He felt like saying, "You should see the other guy."

The priest took him to a room with four other students, all of whom came to the dance drunk and now sat puking into buckets, waiting for their parents to come pick them up. Mick listened intently as Father Devlin called his father. He could tell that his Dad was angry. Mick's Dad showed up twenty minutes later with a mean scowl on his face and told the priests, "Oh, he's going to pay for this." Mick was scared and confused. He thought his Dad had always said not to let anyone push you around. Now, he was going to rip him a new one as soon as they got out the door?

They hit the outside air. His Dad walked down the first two steps without saying a word and stopped dead. *Here it comes*, Mick thought. His Dad turned and asked, "So, did you win?" with a devilish smile. Mick's boys were standing down by the car and had told his Dad the whole story. Mr. McKenna was proud that his son had stepped up to protect the girl and he took the boys out for some late night pizza, regaling them for hours with stories of his own battles as a young man.

Mick heard two days later that one of the McNamara girls saw the guy he fought the day after the dance and he had a broken nose and forty stitches in the back of his head. Mick felt terrible when he heard this but from that day on he never had to fight again. He was officially a bad ass. The day after that fight he had a lump on his head about the size of the one he had now.

Mick got dressed and headed down stairs with no plan to explain his injury. A few of the cousins, Jillian, Big Tom, and some others he did not recognize were scattered around the living room, most nursing serious hangovers. Big Tom, having already been briefed by Jillian on the night's events, yelled out, "Hey everybody, it's Rocky McKenna!" For the rest of the day he endured pokes and jabs like, "That Apollo Creed's got a mean right cross," and "Yo! Adrian," and "Cut me Mick, cut me." Apparently, Rocky Balboa was a hit in Ireland too. He didn't mind the ribbing. In fact, it was hysterical listening to someone with an Irish accent try to mumble and slur like Sylvester Stallone. All he could do was laugh, but his head still hurt like hell.

Chapter 11

Mick, Big Tom and Mrs. O'Neil spent the next six days relaxing by the seaside at the campsite without any further incidents. Everything was quiet and calm compared to the first night in town. The days had no schedule and the vacation seemed to have no itinerary – much different than any vacation he had ever been on in America. The real purpose just seemed to be for the O'Neils to get out of town for a while, break up their usual routine, and spend some real quality time with the people in their family that they loved. Everyone in the small town seemed to know they were there and it seemed like every person from the village had stopped at the hotel during the week at one time or another to sit and have a cup of tea and just talk with them for an hour or two to get a bit of their *craic*, which Mick eventually learned was Gaelic for sitting and enjoying someone else's conversation and company. It was very simple and amazing to watch. Life slowing down for people to enjoy people. Mick usually just sat back and listened, at least when the accents weren't too thick for him to understand, and took in the pure joy all of the friends and family seemed to take in each other and each other's lives. A lot of the characters he met were some of the friendliest and funniest people he had ever met and they all took a genuine interest in him and seemed to consider him family based simply on the mere fact that he was there with someone they loved. He was seeing first hand why the Irish had the reputation of being some of the nicest people in the world.

Jillian usually had about 3 or 4 hours of office work that she needed to do each day and while she was doing that Mick chipped in by doing whatever leftover chores needed to be done. Auntie Mary sent him into town to buy some supplies on two occasions and he ended up with trash duty a couple of times. He didn't mind the work at all since it made him feel that at least he wasn't a total freeloader. Other times, he slipped down to the docks and sat watching the ships come in and the workers on the fishing boats some more. Big Tom and Mrs. O'Neil spent most of the days catching up with friends they hadn't seen since the year before and seemed to be smiling a whole lot more than they did when they were back in Belfast. And, of course, the teapot was never off the stovetop.

Mick and Jillian got into the habit of slipping down to the dunes for lunch every day, where they would kick off their shoes and share a few sandy sandwiches as well as their thoughts and feelings. Mick had never spoken much of his feelings about Sarah's death and what he was going through but for some reason he could with Jillian. It was like the therapy his parents had begged him to get but which he had refused. Every day they talked for hours. Mick was able to talk to her about how lost he felt, how he didn't exactly know where his life was going from thereon out, how he felt like he had lost everything, his nightmares, and how he sometimes felt on the verge of completely losing his mind. He confided that he felt alone in the world except for the O'Neils and Jillian – people who were complete strangers to him just months before.

Jillian confided that she didn't love Robbie at all, how she was searching for a way to end it, and that she merely felt sorry for him because he had no real family. She just didn't have the heart to crush him by breaking off the relationship at the moment. Both she and Robbie knew there wasn't really anything there anymore and each knew they were only going through the motions until the inevitable happened and Jillian ended it. She was just waiting for the right time. Jillian spoke of how she believed in the concept of a soul mate and how much she longed for someone to spend the rest of her life with. Her Mother and Father were best friends and she saw the same in Big Tom and Mrs. O'Neil. She wanted the same in her life and, although she had many suitors over the years and a few proposals, she would never settle for anything less than that. She would rather be alone than be married to someone she did not love with all her heart. Frankly, she hadn't really been interested in any man in years. Although she didn't directly say it to Mick, it was clear that she was very interested in him.

The attraction between Mick and Jillian that first night, and the awkwardness of the near kiss, hung in the air initially and was quite palpable. Eventually, they talked about it openly and the fact that acting on their physical and emotional attraction to one another just could not happen. Still, on a couple of occasions, they held hands and hugged each other on the beach under the guise of keeping warm during a gusty wind or rainy drizzle, but they both knew it was just an excuse to feel the comforting touch of one another. There was nothing real sexual in it, and although the chemistry between them was very strong and obvious, there was a line they would not cross. They realized they could and would control the urge to kiss and take things further. So, their friendship grew even stronger, and each learned more and more each day that they needed the other to talk to and that there was something wonderful and special emerging between them.

On the day Mick, Big Tom and Mrs. O'Neil were set to head back north, Mick stopped by Jillian's office and popped his head in, shaking a thermos full of tea.

"One last time before we go?" he said.

Jillian smiled almost sadly, shook her head "yes" and grabbed her cardigan off the chair without saying a word. Once they were down the path and around the first dune, Mick took her by the hand and led her toward the ocean's edge. They both stared straight ahead at the cold Atlantic as the wind blew the sand around at their feet, while they took turns sipping tea from the thermos lid.

They stood for a while in silence and began to walk down the beach holding hands. As they reached the top of the jetty where they had stood the first day they met, Mick grabbed her other hand so they were face to face, took a breath, brushed a curly dark lock of hair from her face, looked deeply into her beautiful blue eyes and said, "I just want you to know that I have some real feelings for you. I don't understand what they mean but I just want to tell you how special you are to me and how much I have needed what we have had this last week because you have helped me in ways you will never know." He didn't say it but she had helped him see the value in continuing life, see that there was still beauty and love in the world and that life someday could be amazing for him again – he just didn't know when.

"You've given me hope that I can be happy again and made me realize that I can still have a life worth living.

I can't run away from my life. I've got to go home and try to piece things together. I just want to say this now because I don't know if I'll ever see you again."

His eyes began to tear up and Jillian said, "I know. You don't have to say it," pulling herself into him and putting her head on his chest so as to hide the tear she was wiping away. Although she too did not speak it, the flame of hope in her had also been rekindled. As they embraced and the waves crashed against the jetty, Jillian slipped a note into the pocket of Mick's jeans explaining just how she felt about him and asking him to call her whenever he needed her again.

Chapter 12

HERNDON WAS DEAD and the Feds had no other connection to the U.S. source of the weapons and guns. So, at Maxwell's direction, agent Jensen continued to focus on the dead man, their only lead. Jensen and two other members of the Unit interviewed every tenant in the building and got the same response from everyone. No one knew Herndon but a few had seen him. He was only there a month and kept to himself. Jensen scoured hours of surveillance tape from a nearby 7-11 to see if Herndon ever used the phone there. He found nothing. He had the phone records from the lobby of Herndon's building but the collection of numbers meant nothing since there was no way to determine which numbers, if any, he had dialed. There were hundreds of long distance calls of various lengths to all parts of the United States. Jensen checked the post office for rented postal boxes and every coffee shop, liquor store and bar within two miles, but came up dry. The building manager had produced a copy of Herndon's fake license but told Jensen he didn't think Herndon had a car. On a hunch Jensen checked the local car rental agencies. Economy Car Rental three blocks away had record of a John Herndon renting a Ford Escort two weeks before the raid at the Brooklyn docks. The rental contract indicated the mileage when the car left the Economy lot and the mileage when it was returned nine hours later. Herndon had traveled exactly 456 miles. Since the car was returned nine hours after it was rented, it seemed as if Herndon went somewhere and came right back. He had checked the "yes" box next to the question, "Going out of state?" It wasn't much of a lead but it was a place to start.

Jensen pulled out a ruler, checked the legend on the bottom of his wall map, calculated the inches to come up with exactly 219 miles, the one way mileage from Brooklyn, then stuck the point of his compass as close to Herndon's apartment as he could and began to draw a circle. The circular line he traced on the map crossed near the Maryland/Delaware border, came up through central Pennsylvania, cut through the middle of New York State, and curved down directly through the city of Boston Massachusetts. None of the other places had ever been a hot bed for IRA activity, but Boston was teeming with Irish-Americans and Irish immigrants who were on the Unit's radar. The timing matched too – Brooklyn to Boston was an eight and a half hour ride roundtrip and Herndon had been gone a total of nine hours. He certainly could have headed to Boston and back.

Jensen started by running a search on the computer, cross matching all suspects with connections or sightings in Boston *and* New York City. Over eleven hundred names were found. The results were way too broad to be remotely useful. Jensen then limited the search to Tier 1 and Tier 2 suspects only. A hundred and twenty-five pairs of names popped up. *Still too broad a field to run down on just a hunch*, he thought. He modified the search further and limited it to family member connections for targets in the two cities. Six connections popped up onto the screen. He read the first three files and searched for any updated surveillance reports on the first three pairs of names. Only one had recent activity and the status update reported nothing suspicious. The fourth pair of names had a report attached to it. Jensen clicked on the icon to open the report and a Memo entitled "Fergus Magee/Maggie Magee" appeared on his screen.

Fergus Magee, a Brooklyn-based IRA sympathizer whose name appeared on the Unit's watch list had a sister, Maggie, who lived in Boston, Massachusetts. Jensen scanned the report quickly. The agent assigned to randomly check in on and follow Fergus had uploaded a routine locate report to the system two days prior indicating that Fergus recently visited his sister in Boston for four days. Other than documenting what appeared to be a routine visit to his sister, the report was unremarkable.

Jensen pulled Maggie Magee's phone number from watch list contacts binder on his bookcase and compared it to the list of numbers called from the phone in the lobby of Herndon's building. There it was – 11:43 PM the day before Herndon rented the car. Someone from the lobby of Johnny Herndon's building called Fergus Magee's sister's number and spoke for exactly fifty eight seconds. Just long enough to confirm a meeting the next day. Jensen checked the date on the rental contract against the report log. Herndon and Fergus were in Boston on the same day. Fergus was in on the Herndon shipment …somehow, someway, he was part of it. Following the dead man had lead Jensen in the right direction after all.

Fergus was a Tier 1 suspect on the Unit's watch list. His involvement was not much of a surprise. He was suspected of gun running to the IRA in 1984 but the feds were never able to get any evidence on him for a prosecution. So, they watched him carefully. Fergus had been quiet in recent years, but was going through a high surveillance cycle. It happened from time to time. A few people on the watch list increased interaction recently and surveillance was routinely increased. Usually, in this time of anticipated Irish peace, it was nothing. The Unit had been watching Fergus and seven of his associates more closely in the weeks prior to Herndon's death. The group had been more active and, although their surveillance level was already at an accelerated level, this connection between Herndon and Fergus would now move "The Eight" as they were known, to Surveillance Level One.

Maxwell sat with Jensen's report stretched before him on the conference room table. The report laid out in painstaking detail the events the Unit had been monitoring and investigating in the Woodcrest Section of the Bronx, where Fergus Magee lived. Woodcrest was probably the most Irish neighborhood in New York City. And in a Borough with a lot of tough neighborhoods, Woodcrest was one of the toughest. The Irish had been settling there legally and illegally since the eighteen hundreds. The culture in Woodcrest was thick with pro-Irish sentiment and even thicker with support for the Irish Republican Army, better known as the IRA. In many parts of Woodcrest, someone wearing a Union Jack or speaking with a British accent could easily have the shit kicked out of him. It was just a fact of life there. Hatred for English rule in Ireland oozed from every corner bar and hang out. Woodcrest in the Bronx, and Woodside in Queens, were active investigative targets for the

Western Europe Counter Terrorism Division. Maxwell's Unit watched Woodcrest carefully and knew all the suspects well. At any given time there were thirty to forty telephone wiretaps underway. The Eight were once suspected of running guns and bulletproof vests to the IRA in 1984 and the unit's mission still involved limited surveillance and activity checks on these individuals on a routine basis. In the past, the surveillance had been much heavier but with the IRA having laid down its weapons as part of peace negotiations over the past year, the suspicious activity of these individuals had dwindled to next to nothing. Still The Eight had to be watched and the Woodcrest community had to be bugged – it was the Unit's mission after all. Now, Fergus Magee was once again number one on Maxwell's watch list.

Fergus and the seven others never met as a group, only in twos and threes and never spoke directly of any gun running. However, a month and a half ago the number of phone contacts and face to face meetings among the eight spiked to levels no one had seen since the mid-eighties for no apparent reason. Every bugged conversation and meeting was severely scrutinized by the Unit but all conversation was normal and seemed like small talk between the friends, the majority of who had come to the United States in the early seventies. There was no sense of urgency among The Eight but the FBI's red flags were going up and the level of eavesdropping and phone tapping had been further increased at Maxwell's order.

Fergus was born in Belfast and was a young charismatic man when the Troubles broke out in the late 60's. As one of the young leaders he played a large part in the uprising and political outcry that led to the many demonstrations and riots that ensued. Fergus himself had been armed at the time and had anonymously killed a British soldier and a policeman in the Royal Ulster Constabulary during the confusion of one of the worst riots when he had been cornered in an alley way. Although the government didn't know he was the one who pulled the trigger, there were too many purportedly pro-IRA individuals in Belfast that knew of his involvement so he ran to the United States on a work Visa just to be safe. Eventually, he applied to for naturalization and became a legal U.S. citizen.

Several years ago, the feds tried to nail him on an interstate weapons transport/gun possession charge after a routine traffic stop at a bridge crossing between New York and Connecticut, but it did not stick. The government knew they couldn't convict him as they didn't have enough evidence, but the main reason they pursued the prosecution at all was to get the opportunity to put him in a room and question him to get some idea as to what he was all about. In the process, they developed a profile on him and realized he was a tough nut who was smart enough to mastermind and control some sort of support for the IRA from the United States. What the federal government never realized though was that he did not trust a single soul who was not directly from Ireland and not directly involved in the Troubles in Belfast from day one – thus, the feds could never and would never get close enough to find out anything about him through normal surveillance means. Right under their noses, he ran guns, bulletproof vests, and explosives to the IRA but no one could ever prove it. Fergus was a professional who never left a trace. While the feds focused on the Ancient Order of Hibernians, Irish Northern

Aid, and other high profile charitable groups and Irish societies who openly raised money for Irish POWs and their families as the possible source of funds to the IRA for weapons, they were just wasting their time. The undercover federal agents who joined these groups learned first-hand that the money raised for Irish cultural exchanges and the families of political prisoners actually went where the groups said it did, not to buy guns for the IRA. The government should have realized that the money raised by these organizations wasn't enough to fund a war anyway – it was just small potatoes. Fergus, and others like him in various parts of the US, were the real bag men, coordinating secretly with wealthy benefactors whose faces never saw the light of day at an Irish event or fundraiser but who secretly supported "the cause" financially. The wealthy benefactors, who weren't even on the FBI's radar, were the real source of money to buy weapons from sympathetic governments like Libya, which also hated the British, but who charged a pretty penny for every gun, missile and pack of C4 they supplied.

Past audio surveillance of Fergus had been unsuccessful. His main hang out was a seedy bar under the El on Broadway, in the two hundreds, near Riverside, less than five miles from Woodside, named The Celtic Cross. Fergus spent every afternoon and almost every night there.

Back in the eighties, on busy nights, federal agents sometimes mingled with crowds at "the Cross" as it was called, wearing wires sewn into their tee shirts and baseball caps trying to get close enough to pick up some good intelligence. Fergus seemed too tight lipped and had no real time for Americans, so he never said much when they were in within earshot. Even when he was drunk and boisterous, he never messed up, choosing instead to whisper at his spot at the corner of the bar or to take conversations into the men's room. Plus, the drunker he got, the harder he was to understand.

The feds then bugged the bedroom, living room and kitchen in the spartanly furnished little apartment he kept in Woodside, but he was rarely there and, when he was, he was always alone so there was no conversation to be recorded. He knew his phone was bugged – he could hear clicks on the line and occasionally the feds would pay him a visit in person as some sort of deterrent, just to let him know that he was being watched. Fergus thought it comical.

Three years earlier, an agent posed as a soda dispenser gun repair man and installed a listening device in the soda gun which rested in a holster at the corner of the bar where Fergus always sat. The device was sensitive enough to pick up his whispers but he never said anything of import.

However, Jensen's team had been all over Fergus and the rest of the Eight for that last month, and two days ago Fergus had finally slipped up. Maxwell began to read Jensen's updated surveillance report, written less than twenty four hours ago which summarized the details.

The report began by providing some background. For the past year, an agent by the name of Glen Reid had been posing as an electrician and had finally been accepted as a regular in the bar, but not in the eyes of Fergus Magee who kept to himself and his own people. The report went on to detail a conversation caught by Reid's most recent surveillance effort, which had intensified since the Fergus Magee-Johnny Herndon connection had been made.

Reid was at the bar three days ago when the light fixture in the men's room blew out. The bartender asked Reid to take a look. Knowing that Fergus would often babble to his friends while locked inside the men's room, Reid said, "Give me a half an hour to get some tools and a new fixture. I'll be right back." The bartender gave Reid forty dollars for the fixture. He left and returned an hour later with a bug, a transmitter, and a new fixture. Reid hid the listening device inside the light fixture that hung in the ceiling of the one urinal, one toilet bathroom that wasn't big enough to swing a dead cat. A small transmitter was mounted between the ceiling joists, hidden by a drop ceiling that looked like it hadn't been touched in fifty years. The conversation transmitted from the bathroom two nights ago was muffled and the only recognizable voice belonged to Fergus. The report ended with "Transcript in dictation."

Maxwell hit the intercom button on his phone for Jensen. "Did you get the Magee tape back yet from transcription?"

"Not yet." Jensen said.

"You have another copy, right?" Maxwell asked.

"I do," responded Jensen.

"Bring it in here," Maxwell ordered.

Jensen walked into Maxwell's office and went straight to the tape player on the credenza. The quality of the recording was poor. Fergus was drunk to the point of slurring and thought he was alone with his unidentified listener:

Unknown: (inaudible)

Fergus: Relax now.

Unsub: For fuck's sake, they blew Sean's fucking head off.

Fergus: Don't fucking bother your head about him. He fucked up and he was taken care of. Fucking Sean Ryan's not the issue here.

Unsub: (inaudible)

Fergus: He's gone now and so are (inaudible) crates. Bigger things are on the rise. The SAMS are on the way from Juarez. Be patient and be careful. This is *our* time!

The tape ended with a toilet flush and the door opening and slamming shut.
"We got him on conspiracy to ship arms?" asked Jensen.
"This proves only that Fergus knew about the AK-47 and grenade shipment. There's s no proof that he was the source or that he had planned any part of the shipment or the killing," said Maxwell.

"Do you want me pull him in for a round of questioning anyway?" asked Jensen.

"We'd only have to let him go. We don't have enough evidence to arrest and prosecute. Plus, you heard him. 'Bigger things are on the way.' 'SAMS,' surface to air missiles are on the way from Mexico," said Maxwell.

He continued, "Grabbing Fergus now would only tip his people off and the missiles would be redirected to wherever they were going to be used. The smart thing, and only real alternative, is to watch Fergus and nail him and his supplier before the missiles reach their destination and innocent people get hurt. I want you on him like stink on shit. Got it?"

"Got it," answered Jensen.

Chapter 13

ON THE DRIVE BACK TO BELFAST, Mick confessed from the back seat to the O'Neils that he and Jillian had become quite close during the week. Mrs. O'Neil turned and laughed as Big Tom smiled through the rear view mirror.

"Do you think no one noticed the connection you two had?" she said.

Mick was shocked. He had thought that they had been quite clandestine about their lunches and walks on the beach. He was very much embarrassed and said, "It wasn't anything like that…"

"Oh no, Mick, I didn't mean to suggest anything like that. I know you and I know Jillian and I know it was nothing like that. It's just that everyone knows what a beautiful person Jillian is and we were all glad to see you have a friend your age that you could spend time with. And from what I could tell, just being able to talk to her seemed to make you happier than we've seen you since you arrived," said Mrs. O'Neil.

"It really did. But how could you see that?" asked Mick.

"There seemed to be a little bit of peace in your eyes this last week, especially around Jillian," interjected Big Tom.

"She really helped me a lot," Mick said.

"Sounds like Jillian – wise beyond her years," said Mrs. O'Neil.

"Thank you for taking me to see your family," Mick said.

"You're our family too, Mick. Don't forget that," said Mrs. O'Neil.

"Believe me – I won't. And thank you for taking me in when I had no idea where to go, giving me some time and a place to sort out what was going on. I'll never forget what you did for me here. But once we get back to Belfast, after a couple of days, I think it's time for me to head back to the U.S."

"We don't mind at all. You take all the time you need, Mick. We'll be sorry to see you go, Son," said Mrs. O'Neil with the honest sound of disappointment in her voice.

Big Tom, with a lump growing in his throat, leaned back and said, "We sure will be sorry to see you go, Mick. We have enjoyed every minute of your company and you'll never know what a blessing it has been for us to have you stay with us and to help you get back to a good place in your life."

None of the three said much after that. The rolling hillsides turned into small villages and then into the infrastructure of the urban area of Belfast as they all stared out the window emotionally satisfied yet somewhat saddened by the fact that their journey together was about to end.

The next few days were filled with no real mention of when exactly Mick would be heading home. He really wasn't eager to leave any time soon; however, he had taken the first step of realizing that going home needed to be his next move. The questions he had about who killed Sarah and why were answered in his mind in some vague general way but still bothered him; however, his initial feeling that there was some sort of vengeance he needed to take had largely dissipated. So, he was just enjoying the slow rhythm of typical Irish life.

Mick was in the sitting room enjoying the *Irish News* when Big Tom walked in.

"Want to head for pint before supper?" asked Tom.

"Absolutely," Mick said, perking up.

"Right then. We just have to stop by at Danny's house so I can pick up my pay," added Big Tom

"Sounds good – but the drinks are on me tonight, OK?" Mick implored.

"Deal," said Big Tom.

Danny's house was a block and half away and Mick followed Big Tom up the steps as he rapped the door. Danny, Tom's boss, who Mick had met at the "Republican" pub a few times with Big Tom, stuck his head out the door and greeted the two men.

"Come on in," he said.

Danny locked the door behind them and Big Tom and Mick followed Danny to the back room of the house, stepping over painting supplies, rollers, and buckets of paint on their way. Passing the parlor in the front of the house, Mick heard and saw through the door that was slightly ajar a group of men huddled around a card table in what appeared to be a very serious conversation. Mick recognized some of the faces as Republicans from the pub. While Danny moved some of the supplies out of the way, one of the men in the room noticed Mick glance in and got up and shut the door abruptly. They followed Danny to the back room. Danny went into a drawer and started counting out some bills while trying to figure out how many days and half days Big Tom had put in since the last time he paid him for his occasional painting jobs.

Suddenly, there was a loud thump and then the sound of a boot crashing through the wood at the front of the house. Mick stood half dazed while four men from the parlor yelled, "Fuck! – out now" as they whizzed past him and out the back door, across the garden, and over the brick wall into the alleyway.

"Run," yelled Big Tom, grabbing and pulling on the arm of Mick's coat.

Mick heard the sound of the front door battered off of its hinges and crashing on the floor as he ran out the back door right behind Big Tom and the other five men.

"What the fuck is going on?" he yelled to Big Tom as the larger man helped pull him over the brick wall into the wet alley below.

"Just run like fuck. I'll tell you later," said Tom over his shoulder.

They stepped over an unconscious soldier who apparently had been guarding the back door escape route but who had been knocked cold and was rolling around on the ground as they ran past him and splashed water in his face while running through the puddles in the tiny alley.

Seconds after the seven men hit the alley way, the soldiers who crashed through the front door were also over the brick wall and in full chase down the alley. Mick heard a bullet ricochet off the corner of the wall just as he made a right turn into the next alley way. As he turned the corner he realized there were two more alleys to choose from and the four from the parlor were gone, apparently having chosen a different ally than Danny, Big Tom, and Mick.

Half way down the alley, Danny tried a door in the brick wall to a garden he seemed to know and the three men ducked inside, locked the door, listened, and prayed. They heard the British accents and the splashing of the standard issue boots moving to the end of the alley and start to kick in the doors of each garden wall and garage they could find.

"We have to get to the safe house," said Danny as Mick stood there dumbfounded. "Let's move."

Danny led the way over the short garden fences in the opposite direction and directed the men to an even smaller alley which flowed to the back of what appeared be an abandoned factory. They climbed up rungs tucked out of sight behind a drain spout and climbed inside.

Once inside all three men fell to the floor, soaking wet, heaving to catch their breath and trying to talk.

"Tom, what the fuck was that?" again asked Mick.

Danny, bent over and out of breath answered, "That was an abandoned house where we had some guns stashed. If they had caught any one of us, we were done for."

"Sorry, mate, I shouldn't have brought you there," said Tom apologetically.

"Holy shit! I can't believe that just happened," said Mick.

Danny, still gasping for air, looked up at Mick and said, "Well, welcome to Belfast my friend."

The safe house was built into a hill and the three men had entered from the rear, straight onto the third floor of what appeared to be an old gas company building. Although most of the windows were boarded up, there were missing bricks at various parts in the wall similar to a military pill box post so that one could peek out to scope the surroundings. Danny checked to see if they had been followed and reported back that all was clear.

"We'll wait here then walk out the other side of the building in a few hours after things have died down. Let's go to the maintenance room and get some water," Danny instructed.

Mick and Tom followed Danny over a metal catwalk at the end of which was a steel reinforced door. Danny and the two other men opened the door and walked down the short hallway and turned into the main room. As Danny turned the corner, an arm wrapped around his throat and a 9MM pistol was pointed at his temple by one gunman while another man with what appeared to be an AK-47 took dead aim at Mick and Tom.

Suddenly, the gunman who had Danny, dropped his pistol to his side and said, "Danny, what the fuck are you doing here? Why the hell would you bring anyone here?"

"Dermot, I'm sorry. The house was raided and the Brits were up our arse –

we had nowhere else to go," said Danny.

"What? So, you lead them here? Are you out of your fucking mind?" yelled Dermot.

"We lost them. They're not on us. It's safe," assured Danny.

"Oh, that's brilliant. Are you a fucking idiot? What the fuck is wrong with you, you fucking moron? You lead the Brits to one of our last safe places and then you have these two idiots following you," barked Dermot.

The gunman with the AK-47 recognized Tom and said, "Tom, you should've known better too than to come here."

"Malachy, I know. But we didn't have anywhere else to go."

Once Malachy lowered his weapon and stepped to the side and Mick was no longer focusing on the barrels of the two guns pointed at him, Tom, and Danny, he noticed that behind Malachy was a blindfolded man about

19 years old tied to a chair and bleeding profusely from the side of the head, mouth, and knees. Apparently, they had walked in on a beating. From what he could tell, the man's kneecaps had been blown off. This was something he had read the IRA did to people in order to teach them a lesson. It was not totally crippling but did cause major problems with walking for the rest of a person's life. Mick wasn't about to ask any questions about what lesson they were teaching this particular fellow.

Dermot realized Mick was looking at the blindfolded man and said, "Tom, who the fuck is this?"

"He's okay Dermot. He's my cousin Mick. His wife was killed by the bomb at the Bethan funeral. He's no reason to go against us on this," Big Tom explained.

Dermot turned directly to Mick.

"Oh, yeah? Well, guess what? See this fucker here? This is one of the loyalist bastards who probably killed your wife! And the fucker also knows who shot my uncle in the head and left him to die on the railroad tracks three years ago. A good Republican. Dead because of this piece of shit. He knows who did it but he's not talking. This fucker knows but he's not gonna talk," Dermot repeated, his voice beginning to crescendo, "Oh, but he's gonna talk. He's gonna talk alright. If it takes us all night."

Dermot's eyes grew big and his pupils widened. Mick stepped back, frightened by the blank expressionless look on Dermot's face that showed he had lost all sense of calm or reason.

Suddenly, a sound like empty 50 gallon drums being knocked over came booming from two floors below. Dermot yelled at Danny, "Fuck Danny. You stupid bastard! What've you done! Open the hatch. Now!"

Danny and Malachy struggled to open the rusty metal hatch on the floor nearby then each jumped down into it. As the first two men disappeared down the hatch on the floor Mick and Tom stood and watched in frozen amazement as Dermot whispered, "This is for Paddy" into the ear of the bound and gagged man, then fired two pointblank shots from the 9MM into the side of his head knocking the chair onto its side, as Mick and Tom gaped at the scene anemically.

After a few seconds, Mick snapped out of his shock and ran to the man desperately cradling his head, trying to stop the blood from flowing. It was no use and in seconds Mick's hands were covered in blood and brains.

Big Tom turned to Mick and said, "Come on. Let's go Mick. We've got to move, now!"

"No, no, no," Mick said staring down, shaking his head, "I can't leave this."

Dermot barked, "Yes you can – he's gone. There's nothing you can do but sit here and take the blame for it since your covered in his blood and you have motive – revenge for your wife – they'll crucify you. Come on, man. Be smart. Move!"

"Down the hatch now," he said pointing the gun directly at Mick, then waiving it at the hole in the floor.

Mick didn't know what to do. He saw flashes of Sarah. He saw himself being arrested for a crime he didn't commit, and he had a premonition of the British soldiers coming in with guns blazing, and asking questions later, if he didn't run right then and there. As Dermot held the hatch open Mick ran over and slid with blistering speed down the slippery metal chute for two stories, landing softly on a bed of cut up foam and cushions. At the bottom of the chute sat a dingy gray Ford Cortina. Danny tried to get in and Dermot waived him away with the gun.

"No, not you. You brought fucking soldiers here, you're on your own – hit the streets and fend for yourself. And if I ever see you again you're a dead man." Danny, looking horrified, said, "No, Dermot, no. Please. I won't make it out."

Dermot ignored his plea and motioned for Tom and Mick to get into the back seat. Dermot sat in the driver's seat while Malachy rode shotgun, albeit with an AK-47.

As directed, Danny began to walk across the vacant first floor with the AK-47 pointed at his back. After one last look back at the car, Danny opened up the bolted door on the other side of the building and walked right into a hail of British gun fire and died before he got two feet away from the door.

In the ensuing confusion, the Ford slowly pulled out, unnoticed from an obscured loading dock near the railway tracks on the farthest side of the building, and headed south toward the countryside.

After about 45 minutes, the Ford was well into the country and near a small town Southwest of Belfast. Tom and Mick looked at each other and sat quietly the entire time without speaking a single word. At the first stop sign they hit, Big Tom leaned forward toward Dermot and said, "Alright Dermot, just let us out here and we'll make our own way back." Just before Mick was able to open the door, Dermot hit the door locks, looked over at Malachy and as the sun set low in the horizon said, "Sorry boys, but I don't think so."

Chapter 14

THE DIRT PATH that led to dilapidated farm house was barely visible in the darkness of the night. For what seemed to be miles, all of the farms, buildings, and fields seemed abandoned. Even the beautiful stone walls that normally surrounded most properties out in the countryside were in disrepair. The area was desolate. High fields of un-mown hay or grass were everywhere. There seemed to be nothing in every direction. The men walked slowly up the path and stopped at the front door. Dermot unlocked the door and the door creaked open.

Inside, Dermot tried the light switch but it didn't work. Using a flash light he searched the dark room and found gas lamps filled with kerosene in various places and lit the two near the fire place. The furnishings were Spartan. A few tables, a couch, a couple of folding chairs.

"Malachy, go check the box," Dermot said as Malachy walked outside with his flashlight around to the back of the house. After about five minutes the lights in the kitchen and one of the two bedrooms in the back of the house came on. Tom and Mick remained silent as Dermot walked into the kitchen and two other rooms to make sure there was no one else there.

Malachy walked back in the front door and fumbled with the antenna of an old transistor radio to find a news station. The four men sat in the living room without speaking, each just knowing that they were merely waiting to hear the news about the scene from which they had just run. After twenty minutes, the headline news anchor's voice crisply described the murder of a twenty year old man who was the nephew of a prominent Protestant politician. Dermot and Malachy looked at each other with raised eyebrows as if the full identity of their tortured and murdered prisoner was news to them. Dermot knew he was a member of the UVF, the IRA's fiercest enemy other than the British themselves, but the fact that he was also politically connected made Dermot grin sadistically. Malachy nodded in acknowledgment of the grin.

The radio voice said that despite the IRA's recent agreement to lay down its weapons in furtherance of the peace process negotiation, the fact that the dead boy was a Protestant who may have had ties to the UVF pointed to IRA involvement. Sinn Féin, the political wing of the IRA condemned the shooting and disclaimed any involvement in it whatsoever. This was no "news" to Dermot and Malachy. They were among those who had split from the IRA when it agreed to lay down its weapons. They were now being called a "splinter group" and had named themselves The New Republican Brotherhood. This war was not over for them and there would be no peace with Britain on what they saw as Britain's terms.

Pointing to a bedroom with two ratty mattresses on the floor, Dermot said to Big Tom, "You and your boy are in there tonight. First empty your pockets on the table."

Mick put his wallet and passport on the table next to Tom's wallet and car keys. Mick had decided it was valuable to carry an American passport at all times after the night the British had stopped him, Jillian and Robbie. He thought proof that he was an American might stave off some level of harassment if ever stopped again. The only real thing of value in Mick's wallet was the note from Jillian which he had found and read with a smile on the car ride back to Belfast.

"Tomorrow, we're going back, Dermot," said Tom.

"I don't think so," came the reply.

"Neither of us needs to be on the run. No one saw us in the house, no one saw us in the gas works, and no one saw us with you. It's safe for us to go back," Tom pointed out.

"I know you for thirty years Tom. Him, I don't know," said Dermot still motioning with the 9MM that hadn't left his hand in the past 3 hours. "I know you are a staunch Republican and I can let you walk out that door without an ounce of fear that you'd turn on us. Even though I know you would never turn on us, he saw me kill the boy. You know that I can't let him go, that I can't leave any witnesses."

Dermot was right. Big Tom supported the IRA but was never one to pick up a gun or plant a bomb. He was a Republican through and through. He wanted the Brits out at any cost and he saw it as a war too, but even though they had killed his daughter, he just couldn't be the one to take up arms. Especially not now, when Britain and Ireland were so close in the peace talks.

Dermot and Malachy were going rogue and Tom knew the high ranking officials in the IRA who had agreed to lay down their weapons just days earlier would not support what happened at the gas works that day. The IRA that Big Tom knew was calculated, only sought out military targets, gave plenty of warning time for evacuations before they ever blew up a target, and gravely regretted any unfortunate civilian casualty of war.

Tom's IRA did not look at civilian death as mere collateral damage. It had a conscious and did only what it had to in order to gain true freedom for the Irish people. Hearing on the radio that the IRA disclaimed any involvement in the execution earlier in the day and that it condemned the actions of those involved only confirmed what Big Tom knew already about the IRA, but it sent a chill up his spine as he sat and realized that he had no idea what these unsanctioned maniacs might decide to do next. Still he had to speak up.

"For Christ's sake Dermot, you're not going to kill him! Catch yourself on," his voice quivering.

"I've no reason to trust him. Not one. And until I figure out whether he dies or not, you'll be going nowhere."

Chapter 15

MAXWELL SAT in the Crown Victoria, parked half a block away from The Cross. He and the other members of the Unit had been following Fergus Magee for three and a half days without gathering any real intelligence at all. Fergus carried himself like a man who didn't care one way or the other that he was being followed. Maxwell was sure Fergus knew that surveillance had increased. Even if Fergus didn't know, Maxwell knew that Fergus would be extra careful since "the SAMS are on the way" and since, as he said, "this is *our* time."

Maxwell had followed enough targets and tapped enough phone lines during his years to know one thing – they all knew they were being watched. They tried to play it cool, then suddenly, when they needed to slip away, they were invisible. It was as if the real shrewd targets did their own sort of surveillance on the police. They would learn where the police or the feds would stake them out, how they would hide, what kind of disguises they would use, where they would be, and most importantly, where they wouldn't be. Therefore, the smart ones used the surveillance process to gather just enough information on shift changes and the habits of the cops so as to devise a plan to get away or disappear whenever he or she really needed or wanted to. It was almost like the target would lull the police into a false sense of security and then disappear into thin air. Maxwell had seen it too many times and he was not going to let that happen here. This time, there would be a full court press.

The Unit had been fully briefed and reminded of the fact that Fergus may be watching the Unit as much as it was watching him, that everything was to be done with pinpoint accuracy, and that there were to be no mental mistakes. The message was clear: if they lost Fergus for even a minute, somebody's ass would be on the line.

The door of The Cross opened and Fergus squinted as he walked out of the bar into the afternoon sunlight. He reached into his pocket and quickly put on a pair of dark sunglasses.

Maxwell had already known that Fergus was about to walk out of the bar and was ready. His undercover electrician, whose cover had still not been blown, had squeezed the silent signal button he carried in his pocket to ready the team outside just as he saw Fergus move toward the door. The undercover agent just sat on his barstool drawing a smiley face in the foam on top of his second pint of Guinness as Fergus walked out.

Fergus had driven to The Cross and, instead of walking to his car, unexpectedly turned the corner and walked quickly walked up the stairs to the elevated train station wearing a baseball hat and a pair of sunglasses to stop the glare and conceal his face. Anticipating this possible move by Fergus, agent Jensen, dressed in street clothes had been assigned to the train platform above and was waiting on a bench for Fergus to arrive. While the target was heading up the stairs, Maxwell radioed Jensen's earpiece saying, "Fergus, coming your way. Out."

As he had planned, Fergus came through the turnstile just as the Manhattan-bound train pulled into the station. The doors opened and Fergus slid into the train car, squeezing past the exiting crowd. Unseen, Jensen did the same three doors down, watching closely from the other end of the same train car.

The ride into Manhattan was short. Fergus seemed relaxed but without notice jumped off at the first stop once the train crossed into mid-town. Jensen smoothly followed but stayed back far enough so that he could radio his position to Maxwell. "He's waiting on a subway platform for another train that'll be headed toward Wall Street," said Jensen.

"Stay on him. Maintain radio silence if you have to. I'll have backup waiting down there. I don't want to risk losing him." commanded Maxwell.

"Roger that," responded Jensen.

Fergus rode the subway almost to the tip of Manhattan and seemed to walk in circles around the Financial

District. He did not appear lost as he walked briskly with a sense of purpose.

After Jensen's last call, Maxwell had radioed the office and had agents stationed at all the subway exits near the Financial District so that wherever Jensen and Fergus emerged from the underground, Jensen would have help to track Fergus. Jensen recognized the two agents from the Unit about a half a block after he came out of the subway. To Fergus, they were just another two downtown businessmen who he never took a second look at. The three agents formed a wide unnoticeable triangle around Fergus and transferred primary responsibility for a visual on him depending on which way he turned.

Jensen was thankful for the help because, if there was a crowd, Fergus walked straight into it. If there was an alley, Fergus ducked down it, and if there was a way to suddenly cut through moving traffic, he darted through it. One agent alone could not have followed directly without being seen. There had to be hand offs to the others and circle backs and circle forwards to remain undetected. The circuitous route and sudden and evasive movements that Fergus took were clearly designed to lose anyone that might be following him. He was definitely going somewhere he didn't want to be seen. Luckily, Fergus never ran and never panicked so the agents were pretty confident he hadn't seen them at all.

Finally, Fergus seemed to reach a destination. He looked both ways, jogged across the street between two taxi cabs and sat on a bench directly across the street from The Bank of New York. The agents watched and watched but all Fergus seemed to do was sit. He did not appear to be scoping the bank, he did not appear to be looking for someone, and he did not appear to be paying attention to anything. He was just a guy sitting on a bench enjoying the day.

At precisely 2:00 p.m., a tall thin man with Middle-Eastern features, dressed in a very expensive blue pinstripe suit, carrying an almost paper thin leather attaché, sat down next to Fergus. Neither said a word to the other, acknowledged the other's presence or even looked at the other's face. To anyone passing by, their total ignorance of one another would have seemed ordinary behavior on a busy New York street, but to the federal agents, the complete disregard for one another's presence was vastly overdone and glaringly obvious. Theirs was more than a chance encounter.

Jensen, squeezed off a few close ups of the man in the blue suit. Still, he knew the photographs would not be much help due to the fact that the man was wearing an oversized set of designer sunglasses that entirely hid his eyes and because he had a thick, possibly false, beard that almost completely obscured his mouth, lips, chin, and entire facial structure. Jensen took the shots nonetheless.

About two minutes after sitting down, the suit inconspicuously took a tiny white envelope out of the breast pocket of his coat, held it under his hands on his lap for about five seconds, placed it on the bench in the small space between the two men, then got up all in one motion and slowly walked away.

Jensen had been describing the entire scene to Maxwell via radio when Fergus picked the envelope up, slipped it into his coat pocket and started walking uptown.

"Split the team! Jensen take Fergus, all other agents follow the suit. We need to know who that is," commanded Maxwell.

Jensen followed Fergus all the way back to The Cross while Fergus used the same circuitous type path. Once Fergus came down the train station stairs, he simply got into his car and drove off. Maxwell was waiting in the Crown Victoria as Jensen ran down the stairs and jumped in. They followed Fergus home to his grubby little apartment, where they continued their endless stakeout, waiting for some sort of break or slip up, wondering what the handoff was about – what was in the envelope.

After an hour of sitting outside the apartment, Maxwell's radio finally squawked, "SAC Maxwell, come in" said the voice.

"Maxwell, over," he responded eager for an update on the new suspect.

"Boss, we tracked the man in the blue suit on foot as long we could until he turned a corner on Broadway and jumped into a waiting Town Car. Unfortunately, it sped away before we could get close enough to even get a plate number," said the agent on the other end of the line.

"God dammit!" yelled Maxwell as he smashed the walkie-talkie against the dash board over and over again. Jensen sat silently as the pieces of walkie-talkie flew around the car. Maxwell didn't stop smashing the handheld until the only things hanging from his hand were the wires that used to be inside it.

Inside the apartment, Fergus opened the white envelope. He read its contents carefully and then held the instructions from his new Libyan friend over the flame on the stove until the paper burned to ash.

Chapter 16

THE MUSTY OLD BLANKETS in the farmhouse barely gave enough heat to keep the chill out of the cold night air and Mick hardly slept a wink as he pondered making a run for it in the darkness of night. The decision not to run, at least not yet, was easy since he heard Dermot and Malachy whispering or at least moving around from time to time in the next room most of the night. He figured at least one of them was staying awake to keep watch in case he tried to escape.

As the sun came up Mick listened through the wall while Dermot talked on a phone in the kitchen and said to someone on the line, "I'll see you when you get here then. Okay, right."

Mick stretched his leg over to kick Big Tom awake. Since Tom's life was apparently not in quite as much jeopardy as Mick's, Mick understood how he was able to sleep in this situation.

Tom grunted at the kick, then rolled over and rubbed his eyes. Mick was sitting up on the mattress.

Mick leaned over and whispered, "If we stay put, we're dead. How the fuck are we going to get out of here?"

"I'm not sure about that. Maybe they'll come to their senses and just let us go. I've known Dermot virtually my whole life and although he's always been a wildcard, I've never known him to be a killer," said Tom in a low voice.

Thinking out loud and scratching his head, he continued, "But then again, I've never been privy to who did the IRA's dirty work. I never knew it, but it makes sense now after what we saw yesterday. He's always had that sort of "hard man" reputation and has always been high ranking as far as I knew. Everyone always gave him a wide berth, if you know what I mean."

"Are you saying he's an IRA hit man?" asked Mick.

"I reckon he is. But he's got to be with a splinter group now since the IRA decommissioned its weapons. Why else would they basically disown him on the radio yesterday?" Tom wondered aloud.

"It doesn't matter who the hell he's working for right now, I'm his next fucking target!" Mick said a little too loud.

"Think about it. Even if he is a hit man, if he wanted to kill you, you wouldn't have lasted the night, right?" Tom reasoned.

"I guess that makes sense," said Mick, taking some sort of solace in Tom's logic.

Dermot's booming voice startled the would-be hostages as he called from the living room, "You can stop your whispering in there girls. Come in here."

Not knowing what to expect, Tom and Mick entered the living room and for the first time saw Dermot and Malachy without their guns in hand. As they passed the kitchen, Mick saw a teapot brewing and a giant bread knife sitting next to half a loaf of wheaten bread.

"There's some tea and bread," said Dermot, smiling as if Tom and Mick were mere reluctant house guests at some run down bed and breakfast. Mick and Tom fixed some tea and scoffed down the bread with some butter.

In the morning light and without the gun, Dermot didn't seem to bear the persona of a killer and acted somewhat affable and friendly while they ate. Mick noticed fresh mud on the floor and a rolled up paper bag which indicated to him that either Dermot or Malachy had gone out earlier in the morning, possibly to a sympathetic house nearby to get some supplies. Dermot didn't wait long to get right into the topic that was on everybody's mind.

"What is it that we will do with you Mick McKenna?" he said, clearly enjoying the role of hostage taker.

Mick was not sure how Dermot knew his last name as neither Tom nor Mick had offered it at any time. Apparently, just Tom's description of Mick as the husband of the funeral car bomb victim was enough for Dermot to get some details from whoever he had spoken to earlier in the morning while on the phone. Mick didn't answer as he was relatively sure it was a rhetorical question.

"You see, we have two options. I either kill you dead, right here, right now, or you stay with us for a while until we figure out how we can bind you to us forever, in a way that makes sure you'll never turn. Maybe you help us pull a job, rob an English bank, bomb a barracks or anything else we ask you to do. The point is this – if you want to live, you'll do whatever it is, or I use you for target practice."

It hadn't taken long for Dermot's killer persona to return. Mick just glared back at him. There was no way he would do any of the things Dermot described but he was smart enough to know that this wasn't the time to get into yes or no answers. He sat stoically and acted as if his silence meant acceptance.

"Right, then," said Dermot, seemingly satisfied. He continued, "Tom, you can leave in the morning with Malachy. Call Mrs. O'Neil and tell her not to ask too many questions, stay in the house until you are back, tell no one you are missing, and then you will arrive home safely tomorrow. Tell her if she does anything other than that, there will be a problem."

Big Tom picked up the phone in the kitchen and did exactly as he was told as Dermot listened close by. Mrs. O'Neil cried when she heard her directions, but she, Tom, and Dermot all knew that she would follow her orders to the letter or Big Tom would never darken her doorstep again.

Chapter 17

THE NEXT MORNING, a black Peugeot pulled up the dirt road and parked behind the farmhouse. Mick watched from the window as Dermot walked out and shook hands with a well-dressed handsome man in his late 50's. The man wore an expensive brown blazer with a thin black turtleneck underneath, neatly creased tan slacks, and leather shoes which shone in the morning sunlight. He was of average height and build, had a perfectly quaffed head of wavy bright white hair, and a gleaming Irish smile, which he flashed during the handshake with Dermot. His style and the way he carried himself brought to mind the image of a politician or a successful businessman. The sight of him so kindly shaking the hand of a cold-blooded killer was odd.

The man walked up the path towards the house as if he had been there before and Dermot walked behind. Dermot's countenance during the handshake, the way the man appeared to be talking at Dermot, and the way Dermot followed the man up the path revealed a level great respect and deference. It was obvious that the man was a leader.

As the men approached the door, Mick took a seat on one of the folding chairs and waited. The man entered the room, smiled, nodded his head to

Malachy, and walked straight over to Mick and Big Tom.

Smiling, he bent forward, extended his hand and in a strong but polite voice said, "Good morning, Mick. I'm Michael. Pleasure to finally meet you."

Not knowing the meaning of this man's presence, but feeling anything but threatened, Mick merely responded, "Nice to meet you as well, Michael."

The same exchange took place between Michael and Tom. As he bent to dust off the old couch in the living room, before sitting down and crossing his legs with great posture and poise, Michael turned to Dermot and ordered, "Dermot, please bring in a cup of tea for our guests."

Dermot said, "Of course," and scurried away like a child.

Throwing his keys to Malachy, Michael said, "Please drive into town and get us a couple of weeks of groceries."

"Tom, I know you are heading home this morning so I won't ask you, but Mick – is there anything we can get you to make your stay as comfortable as we can?" Michael asked.

"No, I'm fine. Thanks," Mick said.

Malachy took the AK-47 and slid it in the back seat of the Peugeot before driving off. Dermot remained in the kitchen, as apparently was Michael's intent.

Michael said to Mick, "I am very sorry to hear about your wife, Sarah."

He seemed genuine, so Mick thanked him for his concern.

"I am sure it has been tough for you. I'm sure you know by now, we've all been touched by this in some way. Me, you, Tom, Dermot, Malachy, all of us – or we wouldn't really be here having this conversation right now. It's not our fault that this is the case or that we've had to fight for what is rightfully ours, while they killed our family members all around us."

In a way Mick couldn't disagree with what Michael was saying, *generally*. But the peace on the horizon and the cold-blooded killing of the boy didn't make sense at all.

Dermot came in with the tea and toast and the four men sat around not saying much of anything at all until Malachy returned. The goodbyes were said to Big Tom and Mick knew that he would be safe. Big Tom was someone who knew who he should fear and knew what he had to lose back home. They knew it too, so they knew he wouldn't talk. Michael shook Big Tom's hand on the way out the door too and said, "Don't worry about Mick. He'll be fine. You know his situation with us is a little different than yours is. But don't you worry, you'll see him home soon. You have my word."

Big Tom nodded, put his head down, and got into the Peugeot with Malachy. Mick watched while the dust from the dirt road flew up from the back wheels as they drove down the path and made a right.

For the next week, Mick, Dermot and Michael, sat around the farmhouse, playing cards, telling stories, and drinking tons and tons of tea. Malachy never joined in, preferring to stand guard outside and chain smoke his cigarettes.

Unnamed people came and went under cover of night and Mick soon realized that the farmhouse was some sort of way station for people "on the run." One day in particular, two men with short haircuts arrived at the farmhouse and much to Mick's delight Malachy was taken back up to Belfast to attend to some other task. A polite young recruit named Ruairi, who appeared to be about twenty years old, was left in his place to help keep an eye on Mick. Although always armed and vigilant in his watch over Mick, he seemed friendly, but kept to himself, just as Malachy had done, just without the evil demeanor. Mick and his 3 hostage-takers, Michael, Dermot, and Ruairi, were living a quiet yet strange existence.

Mick was developing a liking to Michael as he seemed to be a very intelligent and learned person. *Maybe it's Stockholm Syndrome*, Mick thought – where the hostage begins to bond with the hostage taker. Or, maybe it was the fact that Michael shared with Mick a view of the Irish history that did not appear in the history books he had read. Or, it could be the fact that Michael often spoke with great insight regarding the historical bias of the history books, which didn't even begin to tell the true and entire story. On this point, Mick had to agree, knowing full well the ease with which those in academia and those with control could re-write history to suit any government's needs.

Eventually, Mick was allowed to walk around outside the farmhouse where he would sit on a stone wall visible from the house and dream of times with Sarah. Ruairi was never far away.

Often Mick would read some of the Republican materials Michael had given him. One of the pamphlets in particular horrified him. It included pictures of suspected IRA members and IRA sympathizers who had been murdered. The pictures depicted the almost unrecognizable battered and blooded faces of those murdered men in their teens and twenties, whose penises and testicles had been sliced off and stuffed into their mouths. Mick couldn't help but notice they were all between 18 and 20 years old, all close to Ruairi's age. The pamphlet went on to claim that the parties responsible for these atrocities were members of the UVF and or the British Army, and claimed that at the very least there was hard evidence to prove that the British Army on several occasions stood by and watched the butchering firsthand after being involved in the tracking and capture of the suspect. Instead of arrest, the English soldiers had chosen to let the UVF exact what it saw as justice. The pamphlet indicated that no one was ever prosecuted for these crimes.

Although Mick had been trying to temper his growing hatred for the British occupation and its alleged coordination with the UVF, these pictures and pamphlets were having a strong effect on him. Although he realized that everything Michael gave him was propaganda, he also knew there was at least some truth to it all and wondered whether he would have joined the IRA as a young man if he were born in Ireland. He wondered if he would have stood by and done nothing, whether he would have ended up as one of the teenagers he saw in the brutal photos, or whether he would have starved himself to death like Bobby Sands just to show the world how little the British government cared about human life. He thought and thought on it but couldn't decide where he might have ended up. Even as he sat on the wall outside a building where he was being held hostage, he still didn't know whether Michael was right or wrong about continuing the fight or the proposed peace plan. He was more confused than ever.

Eight days after being taken hostage Michael asked Mick to take a walk with him to talk. It hadn't taken long for Mick to realize that Michael wasn't there just to babysit him – Dermot and

Ruairi could have done that themselves. Michael was hiding out for some reason. Also, Mick realized that Dermot and Michael were taking way too long to figure out what to do with him. They had a plan in mind and they were obviously just waiting for the right time to come. Maybe he would get a few answers during this talk.

As they walked through the old unused goat paths where grass no longer grew and onto the foothills that surrounded the house, Mick started the conversation, "What are you hiding from?"

"I was wondering when you would ask me that," said Michael with a smile.

"Well, why the hell else would you be hanging around this shit hole with Dermot," replied Mick.

"Let's just say that there are some financials being looked at belonging to some very wealthy people in the States with whom I have had dealings, and if things have not been covered up the way they should be, my door will be the next one to be kicked down. So, until I know for sure, I get to sleep on the dirty mattresses with you two," Michael said, looking to Mick for acknowledgement.

The sun was setting over the horizon and the gloaming had begun. Looking out into the majestic valley as the light magically danced off the green fields, Michael, as if almost in a trance, said in a barely audible voice, "Oh, my beauty. *My* Ireland."

He continued to gaze at the land as if he was looking straight into the face of God himself. His eyes glazed over and his face seemed strained and sullen. It was the same soulless face that he had seen on Dermot right before he executed the bound man in the gas works.

There was no doubt in Mick's mind at that moment that Michael's love of his country was his entire life. Whatever else his life had contained had been taken from him and Ireland and its struggle for freedom was all that remained. That freedom was now Michael's sole purpose in life – without it he had nothing and no reason to live. Mick also stood still, recalling the warped, historical, logical, and somewhat reasoned explanations Michael gave to all this madness. Yet, he knew for sure at that moment that this splinter group, or whatever it was, simply could not let go of the battle. The hatred for the British, the UVF, the Protestants, and anything else that had threatened their path to freedom in the past, could never be forgotten or forgiven by these men. Mick knew that his captors, and whoever was working with them, would never accept peace. Hatred was all they knew. It was all they had left.

Michael noticed him deep in thought. "What's on your mind?" he asked.

"What about the shooting I saw? What about that? Was that necessary?" Mick finally had to ask.

"Excuse my language, but Dermot fucked up royally when he killed that kid. That was not supposed to happen and believe me that is not going to happen again," Michael shot back.

"Didn't the IRA decommission its weapons in support of the peace plan?" Mick said to provoke Michael.

"No true Republican would support that," Michael replied, then paused. He moved closer.

"Mick, this so-called peace plan, the propaganda that the English biased media is feeding to the people...it's a farce. In the end, Ireland will not be free. Another deal will be cut and again we will be beholden to Britain. It doesn't give us everything we want. This land is ours and our blood has been spilled on its soil for thousands of years. They have no right to dictate to us. Yes, the IRA has laid down its weapons. But there are those of us within the IRA that have not, *and will not*, agree to lay down a single gun until they give *all this* back to us first," motioning to the valley, his voice getting louder and louder. "If we lay down our guns, we stand unprotected."

In a near shout, he continued, "The IRA and Sinn Féin leadership have weakened us all by agreeing to negotiate on Britain's terms! We can no longer stand with such leadership. They are not the true IRA! They have deviated from our one single goal. To stop this tyranny! The same goal we have had for 800 years – *freedom on our terms!*"

He took a breath, and then raged again, "And for that, we turn our backs on our own brother Gerry Adams and his foolish agreement to lay down arms during peace talks and continue the fight without them!"

"Look at the history of the world and what the British Empire has done. For thousands of years they raped and plundered every nation under the sun and only left when they were beaten by war and uprising or received too much political pressure from other countries to stay and continue their rule with a fucking iron hand. We will wait no longer. Within a fortnight, history will change and not because of this stupid fucking peace plan but because of true patriots like me and my men!"

Mick let the rhetoric set in.

Michael then leaned straight into Mick's face, lowered his voice to a near whisper and said, "And believe you me, like it or not, you will play a part in helping us, the New Republican Brotherhood, in our glorious plan to change history."

Mick stood stone-faced and glared at Michael until the madman turned his head and screamed out into the valley, "These bastards won't be out until we beat them out! And beat them out we will, *so help me God!*"

Having revealed his rage to Mick and, uncomforted by his loss of his cool and controlled persona, Michael backed off and curtly said, "Let's go," and started walking back down the hill at a fast pace.

Back at the farmhouse, Michael was cold and angry for the next two days. The conversation with Mick on the hill had triggered something in Michael that had been lying just under the surface. There was no further mention of their conversation on the hill or the plan of which Michael had spoken. But Mick had confirmed that Michael was on the run too, that he was the leader of the splinter group, that he was a desperate maniac, and that even the most nationalistic of Irish Republicans had turned their backs on him and the rest of his group. Most importantly, Mick had confirmed that something big involving him was going down in the next two weeks. He didn't know how they planned to use him but he knew that he couldn't just sit around and wait for it to happen.

One morning as Mick walked past the kitchen, he saw a man with a stump for a right arm inside. As Mick peeked through the crack in the door, he saw the one armed man was directing Ruairi, who sat working in front of a box with electronics and wires hanging out of it. Seemingly, the man was a bomb maker who, on at least one occasion, apparently, had managed to blow himself up.

Mick sat still and listened intently as Ruairi peppered the one armed man over and over again about how the bomb would be used. The bomb maker, who needed someone with two hands to build the weapon, was growing impatient with the questions, but assured Ruairi over and over again that there would be no mistakes and that the target location would be evacuated hours before the bomb ever went off. Ruairi put down the soldering iron to indicate that he was not going to do another bit of work on the bomb until he knew the entire plan. Apparently, the police, the British Army, and the British government itself would be notified ahead of time by phone. After about ten minutes of give and take between the two men, it became abundantly clear that no civilians would be hurt, and, in fact, no one at all would be killed. Finally satisfied, Ruairi picked the soldering iron up again and got back to work.

Mick tiptoed back to his room undetected.

The bomb maker was there for a few days. At meals he would eat with them but they never spoke his name and he never spoke to Mick. It was all Mick could do not to stare at the stump while he sat on the edge of the table looking at the chunky bald man choke down a bowl of canned stew.

After a few days, the bomb maker was gone and Mick supposed the bomb was gone too. After having seen the man with the stump, Mick was more afraid of Michael and Dermot than ever as he sat around waiting to hear his fate and looking for a way out. He shuddered to think about where the bomb, which had been made in the room right next to him, would be detonated.

But Mick's mind was finally clear on who these men were. Michael and Dermot did not want peace – even in the light of English withdrawal. These were mad men who could not live without the war. Without the war there would be no place for their hatred. These men killed not to put an end to killing, but for the sake of killing. These men were not freedom fighters like those who died in the 1916 Rebellion. These men were not fighting for civil and human rights like the protestors that were killed on Bloody Sunday. These men were not like those in the Irish Republican Army who agreed to decommission their weapons in the hope of finally achieving The Cause's one true goal of peace and freedom. These two men were animals. They were nothing more than cold-blooded murderers. And he was sure that Michael and Dermot were going to kill him once they were done with him. He'd have to escape soon.

On day ten, Mick sat on the mattress in the back bedroom planning his escape when Michael asked him coldly to come out into the living room.

As Mick entered the room he saw Dermot sitting by the door with his 9MM strapped to his side.

"It's time you know your role," said Michael.

Mick sat patiently waiting for him to continue.

"We need something. And you need to go get it for us. There are watch lists at airports and closed circuit cameras at banks that prevent us from obtaining what we need all by ourselves. Plus we have some unexpected heat lately in the US. We need someone inconspicuous to walk into The Bank of New York and remove the contents of a safe deposit box. We can't take any chance of sending any one of our men in to get it and you're a squeaky clean American. You get the contents of the box. You give it to our man in the US, and you walk free. It's very simple. We never see you again and you live life happily ever after. Look at it as your small part in getting something we need for us to get revenge on those who are responsible for killing your wife, doing something for Ireland, and saving your own life in the process," said Michael.

"Go fuck yourself!" yelled Mick.

"I won't do it," he reiterated.

"Oh, yes you will," Michael said calmly and motioned toward someone outside the window.

"You'll have to kill me first," Mick said.

"Not exactly," said Dermot as he flung the front door open and Ruairi pushed Jillian into the room, down onto the floor, gagged with her hands tied behind her back.

"We'll kill her first," Dermot said.

Dermot had found the note from Jillian in Mick's wallet the first night at the farmhouse and anticipating Mick's refusal to cooperate, tracked her down using her phone number and his contacts at the phone company.

For a second, Mick stood in shock at the sight of Jillian bound and gagged then screamed, "You bastard!" as he lunged toward Michael.

Ruairi easily intercepted him and smashed him across the chin with the butt of the AK-47, causing him to crash to the floor near Jillian. Mick crawled over to Jillian and held her tight on the filthy floor as the gunmen above them watched without expression.

Chapter 18

ONE THING MICK KNEW FOR SURE was that once he got Dermot and Michael what they wanted, he and Jillian were dead. He knew for sure when, upon leaving to start his mission, they hadn't even bothered to blind fold him as they drove him away from the farmhouse and to the airport. It didn't matter to them if he knew where they were because they knew they were going to kill him as soon as he gave them what they needed. His captors knew that in the darkness of night on the day they had brought him to the farmhouse there was no way Mick could have known where he was, but they should have been worried about him going to the police with directions back to the farmhouse once he went through airport security on his mission and was free at last. Yet, they hadn't cared at all. Unwittingly, they had confirmed his suspicion that they would kill them regardless of what they had said. That was their first mistake.

As Dermot silently drove, Mick took exact mental notes of every right and left turn they had made, every landmark he had seen, and the name on every one of the infrequent street signs along the way – at least until they were on the highway. He took note of the elapsed time using the dusty digital clock on the car at each turn. Once out of the countryside and on the highway seeing signs for the airport, he took one last note of the exit name and number, closed his eyes and worked the direction backwards and forwards in his mind over and over again until they were locked there forever. Jillian's life depended on it.

The ride to the airport had taken exactly 38 minutes without traffic according to the clock in the Cortina. Just before Dermot walked Mick up to the security gate where he would release him and could go no further with the gun he had in his pocket, he handed Mick his wallet, his passport, and a small carrier-on suit case, saying, "Take this, there's nothing but a big coat in it but you'll look out of place without luggage. And remember, you don't end up on the other side to meet our man, we won't hesitate to kill her. She means nothing to us. Remember that."

Mick just turned and headed toward security. Once through the security and passport checkpoints, he found a magazine store where he bought a notebook, a pen and a detailed road map of Ireland. His flight wasn't for another hour, so he spent the time sitting at the gate mapping out his way back to the farmhouse. Since they were going to kill them the second Mick turned over the information, the rules from here on out had to be on his terms. There would be no turnover in the US. Although his captors didn't know it yet, once he had the information, they wouldn't get a thing until he took Jillian's hand and they walked out of the farmhouse unscathed.

On the early morning flight to New York City's JFK Airport, Mick opened the note Dermot had given him describing the man who would pick him up and detailing the fact that the man would be standing with limousine and taxi drivers holding a sign with the name McKenna on it once Mick came through customs in the US. Dermot's note also had the phone number to the farmhouse on it that Mick was to call once the deed was done in order for Jillian to be released.

As he stared out the window at the clouds and scribbled notes on the notebook he had bought, Mick racked his brain for his options. He knew he had to get back to Jillian to make the exchange, but he didn't know what to expect once he landed in the US, so devising a plan was difficult. All he had to go on was the fact that he would be picked up by the man, who Mick was sure would be armed, and that he would be taken to a bank. Other than that he knew nothing other than he needed to somehow get the information away and somehow buy time so that they wouldn't just shoot Jillian the moment he escaped. Mick knew he had to take whatever was in the box and make a trade no matter what – there was no other way around this fact. Over the course of the next four hours, he developed and scrapped so many plans that his mind was spinning. Finally, about an hour before landing, he had it. The plan was simple once it had come to light. He asked the stewardess for a Jameson with tons of ice, reclined his coach chair, and relaxed in his seat for the first time in weeks. After touch down, things would get interesting, but for the next hour, he would rest and relax. He was going to need it.

Chapter 19

AFTER THE FLIGHT LANDED, Mick stood up and pulled his carryon out of the overhead. He opened it up and put on the puffy green army jacket that made him look about twenty pounds heavier than he was. He exited the plane, set his watch to 9:12: a.m., went through customs and, as directed, smiled but never spoke a word to the agent who said, "Welcome home, Mr. McKenna," as he stamped his passport.

Mick walked through the customs gate at JFK and on his right stood a gaggle of limousine and private car drivers holding signs. He saw a skinny ragged looking man with straggly grey shoulder length hair holding the sign with his name on it. Mick walked over to Fergus Magee.

After making eye contact and each nodding, Fergus put his hand in his coat pocket, looked straight into Mick's eyes, then down to the pocket, then back into Mick's eyes and nodded again. Mick smiled and said, "Of course" acknowledging what must have been the international sign for "I have a gun in my pocket and if you make a scene here, I will shoot you."

Fergus escorted Mick out to his car in the short term parking lot. As they got to the lot and out of the sight of most on-lookers, Fergus got close enough to Mick to jab the gun into Mick's back, through his pocket, in order to direct him towards the right vehicle and to let him know that there was to be no funny business here.

Mick got into the passenger seat of a beaten up Chevy Bel Air. Neither Mick nor Fergus saw Agent Jensen shadowing their every move. As the Bel Air exited the airport parking lot Jensen followed at a safe distance and radioed back to headquarters to update Maxwell on Fergus's meeting with the new man. Agents at the command center immediately started working JFK contacts and U.S. Customs for a name. They'd have an ID shortly.

Trying to get a feel for his new captor Mick jumped right into it, "What do you get out of all this?"

"Well, son, that's something someone like you will never be able to understand. Just shut your gob and do what you're told and never you mind what my fucking motivation is, alright!" Fergus replied abrasively.

This guy was as hardcore as the rest. Although he lived in America, the man still had the thick Belfast accent Mick had learned to notice so easily. He spoke just like Big Tom but certainly wasn't as polite.

They drove for a while towards the city and Fergus kept looking over at Mick with a look of confusion on his face. Something was bothering the man and Mick finally asked, "What?"

"Why the hell would you ask me 'what's in this for me?' Who the fuck do you think you are asking *me* that sort of question? You should just sit there and shut the fuck up. What do you think – you're going to change my mind? …that you're going to get out of this somehow? There's a job to be done, Son, and you're prepared to do it or else, right?"

"Right. I realize that. But something Michael said to me has me wondering about you," Mick replied.

Fergus was taken aback.

Mick continued, "He said we all have been touched by the killing hand of Britain – even me, as I'm sure you know by now. That's all. I was just wondering what happened to you."

"Well, it's none of your fucking business," he hesitated, "But if it makes it any easier for you – my mother was among the poor bastards massacred on Bloody Sunday, my cousin was tortured and butchered by the UVF, my father was in Long Kesh for 17 years for things he never done, my family was kicked out onto the streets with four wee children and our house given to a Protestant family by the English government…And a whole lot of other shit that I could list for hours to you – is that enough? Is that enough for me to want some fucking revenge? Is it? Is it?" he barked.

"Sorry for asking," Mick said disingenuously and looked away.

Fergus just blew air from his mouth, exasperated from getting himself worked up. Mick had gotten the information he needed in order to gauge what he was up against in this new situation. The man was surely as fanatical as Michael and Dermot.

Once into a part of one of New York's boroughs that Mick did not immediately recognize, Fergus pulled the car up in front of The Cross. "Sit here a minute. If you run, one call and she dies."

Mick nodded. Fergus fumbled with the keys to what looked to be a closed bar. Mick took notice of the street names at the intersection and popped open the glove box to see if he could find something with a name on it. Quickly he found an insurance card and vehicle registration lying under a bunch of receipts and fast food napkins. "Fergus Magee" was the name. Mick stuffed the insurance card in his pocket and slammed the glove box shut as Fergus came out of the bar, put down the very large and seemingly very heavy black duffle bag he was lugging, locked the bar door, picked the bag back up and jumped into the car, hurling the duffle into the back seat.

Jensen watched from half a block away, curious about the bag's contents.

"Going on a trip?" Mick said with a smart-assed tone designed to get at Fergus.

"Fuck off," said Fergus.

In fact, the duffle bag was stuffed with $1.25 million in cash that was the fee the New Republican Brotherhood was going to have to pay in order to get the key to the safe deposit box. The white envelope from the Libyan had detailed exactly where the exchange was to be made, but Fergus couldn't risk taking the cash to the airport with him. Had Mick freaked out or caused a scene that ended with Fergus's arrest, Michael had commanded that the money not be lost too and that Fergus bring it nowhere near the airport.

Within the hour, Mick and Fergus emerged from an underground parking garage next to the Plaza Hotel in Manhattan, carrying the duffle bag of cash.

With a remarkably polished and polite tone, Fergus approached the clerk at the check in desk and said, "Mr. Berger – here to see Mr. Ali Ahmed. Would you please let him know we are here? Thank you." The man behind the counter said, "But of course, Mr. Berger, please allow me to call up to Mr. Ahmed to let him know you have arrived."

After announcing their arrival to Mr. Ahmed, the clerk, said, "Room 341, Sirs. Please take these elevators to the third floor and make a right. He is in the suite at the very end of the hall."

"Thank you," said Fergus courteously.

The two men took the elevator without saying a word and Fergus rapped on the door of 341. A thick dark skinned, Middle-Eastern man in a black suit opened the door slightly, saw it was Fergus and then opened the door fully. The shoulder holster with what appeared to be a Glock swung from inside his suit coat for a split second as he leaned forward to close the door as they passed. Once inside, the bodyguard patted both men down for weapons.

The suite was magnificent. The opulence was like that set for royalty or a head of state. Mr. Ahmed was a tall man with a Middle Eastern accent. He was sitting cross-legged in a pair of white linen pants and a black silk dress shirt. As Mick and Fergus entered the room, Ahmed made no attempt to rise and greet them but said, "Good to see you again, my friend. Have a seat. I am sure it is much more comfortable than the bench we met on a few days ago."

"Yes. The demand you made was as uncomfortable as the bench we sat on," replied Fergus.

"What, $1.25 million is too much for the IRA to pay? Money has never been an issue before? You do not desire what we will provide?" Ahmed said looking at the duffle, as if he was trying to see if it contained all of the money demanded.

"This time it is for the New Republican Brotherhood. We have split away from our former comrades. But rest assured, all the money is here," said Fergus, tapping the bag.

"I don't give a shit who it is for, as long as you have my money," said Ahmed in a dismissive tone.

"We need to see the key and cards," said Fergus.

Ahmed nodded to the body guard who had opened the door. He walked over to a drawer, opened it, then slid the Bank of New York deposit key and two small cards onto the table between Fergus and Ahmed. Fergus snapped up the cards quickly but Mick noticed that one had a printed series of numbers on it and the other had the words, "PW TRIPOLI" scrawled across it.

"Just as you need to see things, I need to see the cash," said Ahmed.

Fergus opened the zipper on the top of the bag and began to dump the money on the table. The guard immediately started counting the stacks of hundreds. While he was doing so, Ahmed turned to the guard and said, "Kahlil, do you know what an Irishman is?"

"No," Kahlil replied, smiling as he waited for the punch line.

"It's just a nigger turned inside out," said Ahmed, holding his belly as he began to laugh heartily.

Fergus stood stoic. Mick knew this was not the kind of thing that would sit well with any Irishmen, not to mention someone who had been through as much as Fergus.

"You think I come here to be ridiculed?" asked Fergus.

"What? It's just an American joke I heard. Relax. I am just kidding my friend," said Ahmed.

By the time the last word had come out of Ahmed's mouth, Fergus had pulled a .357 magnum from his boot, shot Kahlil in the chest and blew him backwards, crashing through a glass table.

Fergus then turned to Ahmed, who cowered on the couch.

"I never liked you fucking Libyans," he mumbled as his finger tightened around the trigger and three bullets entered Ahmed's neck and chest. The blood soaked Ahmed's white linen pants and dripped slowly off the light tan leather couch.

Fergus shoved the key and the access card into his pants pocket and ordered Mick to start stuffing the cash back into the duffle. Then, they bolted out the door and down the stairwell into the alley. They could hear sirens as they walked coolly to the underground parking lot where they had left the Bel Air.

Jensen started running from the front desk where he had been interviewing the hotel clerk when he heard the shots ring out. By sheer luck, Mick and Fergus took the stairway at the far end of the hall while Jensen took the closest he could find. Otherwise, Jensen would have run straight into the gunmen as they ran down the stairwell to safety. It was Fergus's lucky day.

Chapter 20

MAXWELL AND HIS TEAM had been following Fergus as closely as possible without blowing cover for the past week. They had watched the visit to JFK stealthily and saw him pick up the man still to be identified. They had watched the trip back to The Cross and had been inside The Plaza when the shots rang out half an hour earlier.

Maxwell now sat in the hotel manager's office scrolling through VHS video tape of the front entrance trying to get a clear picture of the man with Fergus. Surveillance photos from the pickup at JFK were unclear. Jensen and the rest of the team continued to follow Fergus. Stopping what they feared was a large scale terrorist attack on New York City was more important than grabbing Fergus right now for the murder of Ali Ahmed and his body guard who Maxwell already knew were Libyan nationals, suspected of gun running to the IRA. They could always grab him later for the murders. Thus, Maxwell reiterated the order not to take Fergus down. Continued surveillance until they knew more was the plan. Fergus could lead them to the SAMs. At the very least, Maxwell would wait a few hours to see where this went before grabbing him.

"Who is this guy?" Maxwell muttered under his breath as he spun the VCR back and forth stopping on a frame that showed the mystery man's blurry face. Something about this was all wrong. Maxwell's mind was like a photographic data base of all the suspects on the watch list. He had never seen this man before with Fergus or with anyone else. Fergus had never killed before and was escalating. It was all too strange.

Maxwell's walkie buzzed. "SAC Maxwell, please call base, information requested has been received...Over." came the dispatch voice.

Maxwell picked up the hotel phone and called back to the command center. An agent at command advised, "We finally got the callback from JFK. The man Fergus picked up is named Mick McKenna and he walked off of a flight from Belfast two hours ago. He's from a suburb just outside Philadelphia. But get this...his wife was killed in a bombing by the UVF at an IRA member's funeral in Belfast less than a month ago."

"OK. Thanks, get me everything you can find on him, ASAP," said Maxwell as he hung up the phone, intrigued by the American's involvement.

Maxwell knew the SAMs had likely come from the Libyans and did not like the fact that Fergus had killed off his source of future weapons. He wondered if it meant that Fergus had no future need for arms and was planning some sort of suicide mission where he planned on going out with a bang. *But what did the American have to do with it,* he thought.

Maxwell got up to leave with the sick feeling in his stomach that the killing had only just begun.

Fergus drove in circles around Queens and then the tip of Manhattan for over two hours, twisting and turning in directions no one could ever have followed then suddenly parked the Bel Air about five city blocks from The Bank of New York. Fergus was a pro and knew for sure that they had lost any surveillance detail more than an hour ago before they had ever even entered Manhattan. He and Mick were in the clear now. It was 8:50 a.m. Fergus verbally gave Mick his walking directions, the key, and the card with what he explained was the safe deposit box account number.

Maxwell, who had now joined the chase with Jensen's team, chuckled at the sight of Fergus, a wanted murderer, stepping out of the car to feed the parking meter in front of a Greek diner. Fergus was good – probably one of the best they had ever tracked, but the team had kept up, unbeknownst to the Irishman.

Fergus walked from the car into the diner with the duffle bag. Thirty seconds later, Mick opened the door of the car, got out nonchalantly and started walking hurriedly down the street, heading east.

Maxwell had the team split. He took Mick, out of sheer curiosity.

Jensen and two other agents stayed with Fergus. They had already figured out what was in the duffle bag. They had deduced that the bag contained the payoff for the SAMs when they found a bloodstained and banded stack of hundred dollar bills under the gurgling torso of Ali Ahmed's body guard and another similar stack that had rolled under the sofa. Maxwell figured the meeting was the payoff but something went wrong, or Fergus just decided he didn't want to pay. Whatever the reason, it was clear that Fergus was transporting a shitload of cash.

After a few blocks, Maxwell realized that Mick was heading in the general area of the bench where Ahmed and Fergus had met the other day. He knew there were office buildings in the area and that there was a bank directly across the street. Maxwell jogged between two honking cabs to keep up with Mick who was now moving at a fast pace.

Mick reached The Bank of New York just as the security guard was unlocking the door to let the waiting early bird customers into the building. Maxwell could not figure out why Fergus was walking around Wall Street with what had to be close to a million dollars in cash and why Mick was now walking into a bank seemingly empty-handed. Fearing a robbery or some mass shooting, Maxwell radioed Jensen to send two more of the undercover agents his way. He also called for the mobile surveillance team and directed it to drive over to his area.

Jensen received the message and sent the requested back up. Being down to two agents himself now, he needed to keep a visual on Fergus since he could no longer have him watched from all angles. Jensen walked into the diner but Fergus was no longer in the booth Jensen had seen him in just prior to speaking into his walkie. He quickly checked the men's room. "Shit," he muttered, running over to the Mexican man behind the counter. "Where did the gray haired man with the big black bag go?" Jensen growled at the man as if it was his fault that visual had been lost. The man just pointed to the porthole in the swinging kitchen door.

Jensen bolted past the Mexican and several more as he maneuvered his way quickly through the stainless steel tables and shelves, knocking over and loudly crashing to the ground a stack of pots and dishes on his way to the back door, which was wide open exposing the dirty alley which Fergus had just run through. Jensen hit the button on his walkie and set up a triangulated search with him as the point, walking in the same direction that Mick had gone. He had to pick a way to search and this was a good as any. Fergus Magee had lost them again.

Chapter 21

THE SLENDER, FEMALE TELLER led Mick to the private, numbered only safe deposit box. Much like a Swiss bank account, with a mere number and no name attached, no ID was required and anyone with the numbered access card and the key was guaranteed access with no questions asked. Mick knew nothing of such things. Apparently, this was fairly common practice for the extremely wealthy. The teller seemed puzzled by Mick's attire since the extremely wealthy rarely wore puffy brown army jackets. But, she was to ask no questions, thus, she followed protocol and stuck her required matching key into the lock with Mick's and pulled out the long box. She led Mick to a small kiosk with a counter on which she placed the box then slid a red velvet curtain over so that Mick could examine the contents in private.

Mick pulled the curtain tighter to the wall, and then anxiously lifted the lid to the box. To his surprise, the box contained one single item – a 3 ½ inch computer disk, which instead of being made of cheap plastic and having a white label to write on, was made of silver metal, etched with what appeared to be Arabic words. Mick stuffed the disk in his front pants pocket and walked back into the lobby of the bank, leaving the box in the kiosk.

Fergus reached the Bank of New York and got into the transfer car that one of his associates had parked on the street around 5:30 that morning.

Jensen's men had lost Fergus but he had radioed ahead to tell Maxwell to be on the lookout. Maxwell's team watched as Fergus slipped into the black sedan with the duffle bag. Fergus had calculated no more than a ten to fifteen minute transaction since Mick would have been one of the first in. Fergus waited about five more minutes before he began to worry. He looked down at his cheap digital watch which read 9:19 a.m. Mick should have been out by now. Something was wrong.

Fergus canvassed the area. The front door of the bank was clear. The alley on the side of the bank had a lift truck parked in it delivering cases of beer and wine to the backdoor of a fancy downtown liquor store. Then he saw them. There was a bum rummaging through a trash can who kept looking at the door of the bank as he pretended to dig for some leftover breakfast. On the bench where Fergus had sat earlier, a man in a suit sat reading the Wall Street Journal, whispering ever so slightly into the lapel of his wool suit. In his rear view mirror, was a non-descript gray van with a blacked-out side window, which Fergus imagined could have been used for surveillance. On the corner across the street, was what appeared on the surface to be a city worker in a yellow reflector jacket picking up trash with a stick that had a nail on the end of it. As Fergus stared more closely he could see the outline of the agent's shoulder holster under the reflector jacket. By the shape of the bulge, Fergus figured it was a Glock.

Somehow he had not managed to lose the Feds before he and Mick parked in front of the diner a half hour earlier. It was clear they had followed Mick to the bank. He figured they had followed him there too. His fear was confirmed as he looked at the top of the seven story building cattycorner to the bank and saw the tip of two scoped rifles aimed directly at his windshield and at the front door of the bank.

"Fuck," he muttered.

The sedan had been a good way to leave the bank had everything gone smoothly, but now it was useless. The Feds would catch him in New York City rush hour traffic in a matter of minutes. He'd have to make a run for it on foot. With the agents he had spotted on his left, the agents on the roof, and the cops in the van behind him, he knew he was surrounded and was cooked. He sat for another minute. There was only one way out and he didn't want to have to take it but he had no choice. He spent the next two minutes in the car preparing.

Fergus opened the door, stepped out onto the street, walked around the front of the sedan, went to the passenger side door, slowly pulled it open, lugged out the duffle bag, and headed toward the bank, his hand gripping the gun in his jacket pocket, ready to shoot anything that stood between him and freedom. There was no way he was going away for murder.

The teller who had led Mick to the safe depository was now sitting at a desk near the back of the lobby.

"Excuse me, Miss? May I see the manager, please?" Mick said.

"Of course, is there something maybe I can help you with?" she replied very professionally.

"I'd actually just really like to see the manager if you don't mind. It's a very private matter." He said smiling.

"Yes. Please wait here for a moment," she said.

About a minute later, the teller returned and led Mick down a short hallway to a very modern office made of glass walls.

The two men watched the very attractive teller walk away and once she turned the corner, the balding, slightly overweight manager leaned forward, extended his hand and said, "Sir, how can I help you?"

Swiftly, Mick grabbed the manager's hand and bent the arm and wrist around to his side, holding the man's throat in a vise-like grip. "Listen to me carefully," Mick whispered, trying to sound as scary and terroristic as possible.

"I've got a bomb strapped to me under this coat and unless you want it to go off in here, killing everyone in this entire building, you'll do as I say, understood?" Mick said.

The manager immediately relaxed all his muscles and went limp in order to show that he had no intentions of putting up any resistance. "Just tell me what to do and I'll do it. I don't want anyone to get hurt," he said, his voice wobbling.

"That's right. First, get me a marker and a sheet of paper," Mick said, trying to sound tough while asking for something so innocuous.

The manager nervously fumbled around in his desk looking for a marker while Mick made sure he was not pushing any buttons for a silent alarm. He found a black marker and handed it to Mick with a pad of paper. Mick ordered the manager to stand in the corner and the man looked on curiously as Mick scribbled.

Chapter 22

THROWING THE WADS of 100's and 50's into the air so that it would rain cash was easy. Fergus had spent his last few minutes in the sedan cutting as many paper bands marked $10,000 as he could before the Feds decided to charge the car. He knew that once the handfuls of money hit the morning air that the wind would separate them and the crowded sidewalks around the bank would become mayhem with busy commuters trying to grab as much free cash as they could.

His prediction was right. Sidewalks went wild. People started running from every direction, cab drivers stopped in the middle of the street, and pockets and brief cases where being stuffed to capacity as Fergus stood right in front of the door to the bank bending down over and over again and rising up over and over to throw more and more greenbacks as the crowd gathered around him.

Maxwell's men, whose weapons had been trained on Fergus from the second he left the car, no longer had a clear shot. There were several hundred people crowding the intersection and sidewalk.

Fergus ducked down again but this time he didn't come up with a wad of cash to throw. He dropped onto his hands and knees and started crawling around suit pants and high heels as the mob started brawling over the small amount of money still left in the duffle bag. Fergus didn't care at all. They could have it all as long as it gave him the cover he needed.

"Overhead scopes, come in. Target location? Do you still have him? Over," Maxwell barked through the walkie. He himself had no chance of maintaining a visual once the cash was thrown and the throng took over the city street.

"Negative," came the voice through the speaker. Maxwell could hardly hear the voice over the screams, commotion, and honking car horns on the street.

Maxwell knew that no one could have taken a chance at shooting Fergus in the near riotous free-for-all going on in the streets below them. Fergus's move had been brilliant.

"Ground team A, storm the bank; B ground team establish a perimeter and call in NYPD for help on this," ordered Maxwell. He didn't like having to call in the local police but Maxwell needed them now and he knew it.

Mick said, "OK. Now, show me the back door,"

"What?" the manager asked, squinting and pushing up his glasses.

"Just get me out the back door and you all live," Mick said, raising his eyebrows.

The manager hesitated, confused at not being robbed, then snapped out of it and walked through an access door near the glass office. The two walked down a hallway about twenty paces toward the safe. Mick then sent the manager further down the long corridor to unlock the back door.

The manager walked down the corridor and pulled out a key from his waistcoat pocket and unlocked the door from the inside as Mick looked on from the other end of the hall way. Suddenly, the manager faintly heard two gun shots outside the thick steel door. On his way down the corridor, the manager looked over his shoulder and all he saw was the man in the brown army jacket standing on his tippy toes to hold up the notepad he had written on so that it could be seen by the security camera near the bank's safe. The man did not seem to have heard the faint gun shots. The manager hoped the shots had come from the police so he reacted as if he too had heard nothing and walked back down the hallway to the man wearing the bomb.

"Now, go back to your office and sit there for ten minutes and do nothing," said Mick.

The manager scurried down the hall as told. Still puzzled, he gave the man in the brown army jacket one last look over his shoulder as the light of day flashed through the opened door and the man was gone.

Fergus crawled through the last set of legs in the crowd that had grown to the point of spilling into the alley between the liquor store and the bank due to the scattering of the floating cash. Pulling his .357, he ducked under the conveyor between the truck and store that was being used to roll the cases of alcohol in through the back door. He crept along the wall, gun at the ready. The alley was positioned such that he did not have to worry about the rifles overhead. The buildings they were on had no sight lines to where he was now; however, he knew for a fact that there was no way the Feds would have left the back door to the bank unattended and he needed to cross that alley to get away.

Fergus peeked around the corner to the back of the bank and as expected he saw two agents in the alley, hiding – one behind a trash dumpster and another on the first level of a fire escape overhead. The agents could not see him as he was under the truck peering out through the holes in the large truck wheel. It was obvious that they heard what was going on near Fergus out on the street but they were sticking to their position. However, every once and a while they would look up and down at each other as if they were arguing. The crowd was loud but it sounded to Fergus like they were arguing about whether they should leave their position or not. He figured it was to search for him or to help control the crowd that was now in a full riot as the once proper businessmen and women practically gouged each other's eyes out in order to line their pockets with money. It seemed as if the agents reached a decision as one of them bolted down the alley toward Fergus and disappeared into the crowd. The other agent was now focused directly on the back of the door and Fergus could pass by easily. The agent hadn't looked down the alley toward him in several minutes. It would only take about a second and a half for Fergus to slip by. He waited another minute then sprinted by the alley.

The agent guarding the back door never saw him pass by. He never let his attention drift from his main responsibility, which was the back door.

Running hard and looking back from time to time now, Fergus was sure he was free until the alley in this strangely laid out part of Manhattan's tip began to curve. His jaw dropped as he rounded the curve and realized he had made a fatal mistake. It was a dead end. A brick wall five stories high.

Dammit, he thought. He'd been cornered like this before back in 1968 and needed to shoot his way out. He had two choices now: either get up on a fire escape on one of the few older buildings in the Wall Street area and take to the roofs, or go back the way he came and face the lone agent who guarded the back door. Trapped on a roof waiting to be surrounded was not an enticing idea. The one-on-one odds were better.

Fergus crept back up to the alley that ran behind the bank. He peeked around the corner and the agent behind the dumpster was still there. Fergus looked beyond him to make sure this alley ran a long way. It seemed to run for blocks and he could see cars and taxis whizzing by intersections so he knew this was his way out. There was no way he could head back toward the crowd. It was too risky.

Slipping by the alley that ran behind the bank once again, Fergus slipped back behind the truck stealthily. He took out his gun and yelled as loudly as possible, "No, no. Oh, my God, No! Help, he's got a gun, he's got a gun…help someone, help!" in his best bogus American accent. The agent at the dumpster looked down the alley, where he could see the front of the truck. Then he looked back at the door, and then down toward the truck again. He was torn as to what to do. Leave his post or help the person who was in trouble.

Fergus yelled, "No" again and then fired off three shots into the air.

The agent moved out from behind the dumpster and was now standing in the clear right behind the bank's back door, then hesitated. The small hesitation was all Fergus needed. He stepped out from behind the protection of the truck and locked his sights on the agent who was also raising his weapon. The bullet from Fergus hit the agent right between the left shoulder and pectoral muscle and the second was a fatal gut shot.

As soon as the agent hit the concrete, Fergus rushed past him and disappeared into the bustling morning that was lower Manhattan.

As Mick slowly pushed the door open half way, the silence of the fortress-like bank disappeared beneath a flood of blaring sirens and chaotic screams from the crowd around the corner. Confused by the noise, Mick tried to press the door the rest of the way open but it stopped with a thud. Looking down to the ground, he found a man wearing a black suit, with a blown off-shoulder and a gunshot wound to the abdomen, apparently dead on his back in a small pool of fresh blood. A walkie-talkie lay nearby and a gun was sitting in the blood near the edge of the dumpster. Mick knelt down to feel for a pulse but there was none. Mick quickly felt the dead man's breast pocket for a wallet as the sounds of the approaching sirens began to roar. He flipped it open and saw what he expected – a badge. "Fuck," he whispered, dejectedly.

Mick wiped the wallet and the FBI credentials clean with his coat, put it back in the agent's pocket, looked left and right, stepped over the body, and unbeknownst to him, hauled ass down the same alleyway through which Fergus had escaped just moments earlier.

As Mick reached the end of the alley, he traded his Timex to a street merchant for a fake Yankees cap, a tourist map of New York, and a two dollar pair of dark sunglasses. For the moment, he would lay low and find out what was on the disk. He knew it couldn't be good if the Feds were already involved and Fergus was walking around Manhattan with tons of cash, killing Libyan terrorists and cops like he was squashing bugs. But for the first time since this nightmare began, he was about to start giving the orders. The Feds and the New Republican Brotherhood just didn't know it yet.

Chapter 23

MAXWELL WATCHED THE MAN in the brown army jacket hold up the piece of paper, standing as high as he could on his tippy toes so the surveillance camera would get a good look. The paper read, in what appeared to be El Marko Magic Marker: "BRITS OUT NOW!!!" He also watched the tape of Fergus killing agent Jackson, Mick stumbling upon the agent's dead body in the back alley, and particularly the part where Mick stopped to check Jackson's pulse and wallet.

It was clear to Maxwell that the man in the army jacket was Mick McKenna. There was no surprise there. And he already knew that McKenna had been with Fergus just before he went into the bank. He also knew, all too well, that Fergus throwing cash around a New York City intersection could not have been part of a plan. That had to have been a desperate escape measure upon spotting the Feds and realizing he had no way out.

What Maxwell couldn't understand was why McKenna claimed to have a bomb on him, what he took from the bank, and why he would send the message "BRITS OUT NOW!!!" if he was trying to slip out the back door away from Fergus with whatever the two had planned to pick up from the safety deposit box.

As expected, neither the bank manager nor the female teller was able to tell Maxwell what Mick took from the safety deposit box. Maxwell pressed the manager for McKenna's demeanor during the bomb threat, "How did he say it? Tell me exactly…what was he like?"

The manager responded, "Well…he was a little nervous. It was like he was trying to be nasty and scary but it wasn't really in him. You know what I mean?"

"Not really. Are you saying you didn't believe him about the bomb? Did he ever show it to you?" asked Maxwell.

"He never showed me anything, but I believed him, I guess? …it's just, he didn't seem like the type. You know, like criminal-like…he just seemed like a real polite and decent guy. But I wasn't about to take any chances. Plus, he didn't even try to rob us – all he wanted to do was get out the back door and I wasn't about to stand in his way," he explained.

Maxwell sat in the bank manager's chair. He leaned back and stared up at the ceiling in deep thought as Jensen and the bank manager looked on.

The scene wasn't quite right to Maxwell. No robbery. Fergus's panic move in the front of the building. Fergus killing the agent in cold blood while Mick checked the dead agent's pulse to see if he was still alive. It was all wrong.

Still working it all through his mind, Maxwell said, "Let me see that back door footage again."

He watched it again as Mick jumped back, barely noticeably, in surprise as she saw the dead body was outside the door. Maxwell rewound to watch McKenna check the wallet. He checked the time signature on the video screen against his notes that detailed the exact time that the NYPD had been called in.

Maxwell thought, *he has no idea who this dead man is, yet he takes the time to find out even with police sirens going off all around him. Why would he do that?* Maxwell reviewed the subtle way McKenna dropped his head and said something to himself when he opened the wallet and realized it was a cop. On the first review of the tape Maxwell had missed it, but now on closer review, Maxwell saw the air go out of McKenna as he realized it was a federal agent who had been killed.

Maxwell sat forward in the chair and turned his head to face Jensen who was taking notes on the credenza, Maxwell said, "He may not have robbed this bank, but there was definitely a robbery here today."

"What?" asked Jensen, perplexed.

"He robbed Fergus – that's why he was trying to get out the back door," he continued excitedly as he started to put it together in his mind, "McKenna robbed the IRA and he wanted our Unit to know it!"

"How you figure, boss?" asked Jensen.

"Follow me...McKenna didn't know that we were tracking him and Fergus, or cops at the back door would have been no surprise to him, right? Also, why take the time to check to see if it's a cop? If you're a cold blooded killer like Fergus, you step right over the body, just like Fergus did, without a second thought and never look back. He and Fergus clearly didn't want the same thing – Fergus killed without a thought, yet it seems McKenna considered trying to save the agent if there had been a pulse."

Maxwell paused as his mind swirled with possibilities. Suddenly he blurted, "He's not with them! He's against them! Since he didn't know we were already on the case, his note was designed to make *sure* that the police knew the IRA was involved. He knew as soon as he held up that note the FBI would be called in –

likely whoever tracked the IRA. I think he wanted to reach out to us. And now that he saw Jackson's badge he knows we're ready and waiting. Make sure headquarters sets up a dispatch line to transfer direct to me if he calls in. Do it immediately."

The room fell silent as Maxwell leaned back again in the overstuffed leather banker's chair and a small smile started to creep out of the corner of his mouth. This could be good.

Chapter 24

MICK RIPPED THE PAGE from the Yellow Pages and walked out of the phone booth towards the Kinko's Copy Center which was about six blocks away according to his map. The geek in the Darth Vader tee-shirt at the front counter made him sign in and show ID in order to use one of the personal computer stations. At the back of the Kinko's, Mick slid the silver etched disk into the slot on the computer and clicked on the single folder inside. A window popped up on his screen asking for the password. *Shit, it's encrypted, he thought.* For a second Mick panicked and then he remembered that the other card from the Libyans – the one Fergus had not given him before he went into the bank – had the words PW TRIPOLI scribbled on it in handwriting. The PW had to stand for "password." Mick carefully typed T-R-I-P-O-L-I and let out a breath of air as the file flashed open.

Once inside the folder, Mick raced through 11 different files. Some were in Arabic or Russian and completely undecipherable to him but others were in English and some were in English and Arabic languages. He stared at the screen in fright as he opened three documents in particular.

The first was a schematic that appeared to depict two missiles, one slightly larger than the other, according to the numbered dimensions. At the bottom of the schematic, typewritten words that appeared to be Russian were translated by hand:

жара 9К38 Igla личная портативная ультракрасная самонаводя

изыскивая реактивный снаряд земли -воздуха (СЭМ)

9K38 Igla Personal Portable Infrared Homing Heat Seeking Surface-to-Air Missile (SAM)

There were diagrams attached showing how the missiles could be hand-launched or anchored for launching from the back of a pickup truck or a small boat. Mick couldn't tell but they appeared to be larger versions of handheld surface to air missiles he had seen Middle Eastern terrorists shooting on television years earlier.

The second document was several pages long and contained a day long

Itinerary printed on the letterhead of the British Embassy. Prince Charles and the British Ambassador to the United States were its subjects. The Itinerary laid out in painstaking detail the movements of Prince Charles, who was to arrive in New York City in exactly one day to address the United Nations Committee on World Hunger in place of his wife, Princess Diana, who had been killed in a car crash eight short months earlier. The document also detailed the arrival of the recently appointed British Ambassador, Sir Christopher Meyer, via chartered helicopter at LaGuardia Airport just east of New York City and the exact takeoff time and location of the private helicopter that would take him across the East River from the airport to a heliport atop a building near the embassy in Mid-Town Manhattan. Unmistakably, the Libyans had someone inside the British Embassy in order to have obtained such secretly held information.

The third document was written mostly in Arabic but ended with a paragraph written in English that included two number strings marked "Launch Code" and the map coordinates for a location that was approximately a third of the way up the East River.

Mick pulled the already crumpled map from his pocket and shook his head in disbelief as he realized the coordinates directed him to the UN Building.

Mick gazed in horror as he moved to the last page of the document where he confirmed his fears. There he found a map with several small X's, marking supposed launch positions up and down the East River, and a much larger second X, marking a launch position that seemed to encompass the entirety of Brooklyn and Queens. He also found the words "Target 1" were written across the intersection where the UN sat, and the words "Target 2" were written on a curved dotted line that depicted the helicopter's flight path westward over the East River from LaGuardia to the heliport in Mid-Town. Mick could not believe his eyes. From a simple pickup truck somewhere in Brooklyn or Queens, or from a small boat on the East River, The New Republican Brotherhood, with more than a little help from Libya, was going to assassinate Prince Charles, the British Ambassador, and countless other civilians nearby in less than 36 hours.

Mick sat at the computer station frantically racking his brain. His mind whizzed as sat staring blankly at the now dark screen. He was wasting time but he needed to find a way to accomplish the impossible. On the plane ride he had planned the fake bomb threat and the getaway at the bank in order to put himself in a position where he had the upper hand and could exchange the safe deposit contents for Jillian's life. But he had never factored in the need to stop a terrorist attack in the process!

After scheming for well over an hour, he checked his watch, studied the map to see exactly where he was right now in relation to the targets, stuffed it back in his pocket, and then headed toward the front desk. There might not be enough time to do what he had in mind, but he had no other choice.

For just under twenty dollars the geek at the front desk made Mick an unencrypted copy of the disk and printed out a hard copy of the documents, running them through the computer and the printer without even taking a glance at the contents. The price also included the note pad, Flair pen, and three Tyvek envelopes Mick needed.

"What the fuck?" the geek muttered under his breath when he looked up to hand the customer his change and saw Mick bolting for the door.

Shaking his head, the geek pushed the $2.34 down into his jean's pocket and never gave it a second thought. It was just another nut running around NYC.

Chapter 25

AS THE SUN WAS SETTING, Mick looked through the peephole of the Newark Airport Motel 6 and saw exactly what he was hoping for – his spitting image looking back at him. He released the chain and turned the lock. In walked his cousin who he had called just two hours prior. Mick gave a big bear hug to his first cousin, John Delaney, an insurance agent, who was married with three kids and lived in Paramus, New Jersey.

John didn't hesitate to make the drive to Newark when Mick called earlier that afternoon. Mick and John had grown up in the same tough neighborhood in Northeast Philadelphia and Mick had John's back more than once in a tight spot. They were roughly the same build and height but John was a gentle type who played soccer while Mick was the scrappy wrestler who saved both their asses on many an occasion.

John knew Mick was in some sort of serious trouble when Mick called his office and desperately asked that John bring his passport, driver's license, and at least once credit card that Mick could borrow for a few days. Mick promised to explain when John got to the airport motel.

John had been at Sarah's funeral and knew all of the details surrounding her heart wrenching death, but his jaw dropped lower and lower as Mick detailed the events that had transpired over the past weeks, sparing no detail.

John wondered for more than a few minutes whether Mick had gone crazy after Sarah's death and whether this was all some sort of grand delusion. So, he sat, listening and regarding Mick and his demeanor. The calm detailed Mick that was telling this outlandish story was the same Mick he had known his entire life. It didn't take too long until John realized it was all true and that Mick had no alternative but to pose as John in order to get out of the country and back to Jillian. It was very likely that the feds would be watching the airports now that Mick McKenna was missing. This was the only way.

John was relatively sure Mick could pull it off too. In their late teens, John and Mick looked so much alike that kids who John coached in soccer would regularly stop Mick on the street and start talking to him about their junior league games, practices, tournaments, etc… Mick always laughed as the ten-year olds spoke and then just filled John in later.

After seeing John, Mick too believed he could pull it off. John still looked enough like him for Mick to get past security at Newark International; however, he'd have to make some minor changes in appearance – otherwise he'd look too much like himself and he might be noticed even with the completely different IDs.

Mick was in such a state of shock at the funeral he couldn't remember much from that horrible day. It had been a couple of years since they had seen each other before the funeral and Mick had blocked out most of the time at the funeral home from his memory. The stream of people that rolled past him on their way to the casket at the viewing was a mere blur to him now. One thing he did remember was that John, who normally had a full beard, was clean shaven the last time he saw him. Mick remembered that light moment in the somber day when he laughed and teased John saying, "You sure clean up well." So, just to be safe, earlier in the day, Mick bought some shaving cream and a razor, just in case – otherwise the two weeks of growth that he had accumulated while he was being held hostage would have to suffice as a beard. Just as with the hotel, he had paid for the toiletries with cash he took from a MAC machine immediately after his escape from the bank since he knew the authorities could track him with credit cards. The MAC machine withdrawal would put him three blocks from the bank but it didn't matter – the feds already knew he had been there. Now, he was long gone with whatever cash he would need.

John was a little heavier in his passport picture but more near Mick's weight in his license photo. John also had a neatly trimmed goatee in the pictures instead of the full beard or clean face, but he and Mick would look similar enough.

With a few scrapes of the razor blade and a new identity supported by an authentic passport and legitimate driver's license, Mick was confident he could slip by the feds or anyone else looking for him.

After two hours passed, Mick thankfully observed from the motel window as John, sworn to secrecy for the next 24 hours, walked to his car and drove away in the darkness, leaving Mick to check and double check his plan. Mick tossed and turned, playing it over and over in his head for hours on end. It was going to be a long night.

Chapter 26

AGENT MAXWELL'S SLUMBER on the couch in his office was interrupted at 3 a.m. when Jensen from the war room barreled through his office door. Mick had called the main FBI office phone number he found in the Yellow Pages and told intake that he was the man who held up the IRA sign in the bank and that he wanted to speak to the man in charge.

"We have him on the line," yelled Jensen as Maxwell jumped up and rubbed his eyes.

"McKenna?" he asked for reassurance.

"Yes," replied Jensen as they sped down the hall to the war room.

"This is Special Agent in Charge Cecil Maxwell. How are you doing, Mick?" Maxwell said, partly out of breath.

"I guessed you would have figured out who I was by now. I'm the guy on the bank tape," said Mick.

"We know. It wasn't that hard. You basically left us a road map to ID you," said Maxwell, careful to sound cooperative.

"Well, that wasn't exactly my plan, but it worked out all the same," Mick answered.

Mick knew he had to talk fast or they could trace the call.

He asked, "Are you the man calling the shots there? I need to know that or forget this call."

"Yes. You have the right man," Maxwell confirmed.

"Okay. Obviously, you've figured out that I'm not with Fergus or I wouldn't be reaching out to you," said Mick, much to Maxwell's relief.

As Mick was speaking, Maxwell looked over to the techie in the corner trying to trace the call. The techie bent his wrist and moved his hand with his pointer finger in a circle indicating that there was no trace yet and to keep the conversation going.

"Just come on in. We can discuss the whole thing. We want your help. You are not a suspect here. We saw what happened in the alley behind the bank," pled Maxwell.

"Sorry. I can't do that. All I need is a direct phone line to you. Something big is about to go down," Mick said, speaking quickly.

"We know about the missiles," Maxwell offered, trying to stretch the conversation by including another topic.

"You don't know the half of it. Just be ready when I call. It will be tomorrow afternoon. You need to trust me. You'll have enough time to stop it," said Mick.

"Stop what...?" came the question.

"Sorry, got to go. I need the number now! I'm hanging up in five seconds with or without the number," Mick said demandingly.

Maxwell quickly gave his direct line to the war room, then he heard McKenna say, "Be ready with everything you got." Then the phone went dead.

Maxwell looked over at the techie who shook his head *no*. The line trace had failed.

Mick took the phone number for Michael out of his wallet and dialed the overseas operator from the pay phone near Gate 17A. Dermot answered the line on the first ring.

"Put Michael on the line, now!" Mick barked as he stared out the window at the sun rising over the tarmac at Newark International.

Dermot didn't answer and suddenly Michael was on the line saying, "Well, I have to admit, we certainly underestimated the set of balls on you."

"Let's forego the pleasantries, asshole. I'm sure you know the situation by now unless your man Fergus was caught. So, if you need me to educate you on where we stand right now just let me know," Mick said, trying to goad Michael into revealing whether Fergus had been captured after killing the agent behind the bank.

"We've been fully briefed," Michael responded curtly, reluctantly confirming that he had received the bad news about Mick's escape with the safe deposit box contents.

"Good then. You're a smart man, Michael …so you know you as well as

I do that I have the upper hand now," said Mick toughening his voice, then letting out a small laugh as if to say *who the fuck do you think you are playing with here.*

"Whatever's on this little disk is damned important to you or Fergus wouldn't have been toting all that cash around and shooting up Manhattan left and right. I may not have been able to get into it without a password, but you can bet your ass that the FBI could break its code in a matter of minutes. All I have to do is make one call," Mick bluffed so as to get a read on the reaction to his threat and open the door to further negotiations.

"So, what's your play?" said Michael, calmly tempering his anger at Mick's arrogant manner. He was livid but he knew Mick was right. The American had the upper hand, *at least for now.*

"You know what I want," Mick quipped.

"She's yours. Just turn over the disk to Fergus. Tell me where you can meet him and as soon as he calls this line to tell me the disk and its contents are fully accessible, she will walk out the door. You have my word on that," encouraged Michael.

"Not a chance. Your word means shit to me. You don't get the disk until Jillian and I walk out that farm house door together," Mick said confidently.

"Unfortunately, that's impossible," came Michael's retort, "There is time-sensitive material on that disk and unless we have it within the next 12 hours it is useless to me."

"You'll have it well before then, via hand-delivery, but until you let her walk out the door and release her to me, you get nothing," said Mick.

"We need it now or she dies," Michael responded with a tone of finality.

"I'm calling the shots now – I'm about to step on a plane as we speak," said Mick.

"Are you fucking mad? You don't even know how to get to the farmhouse!" Michael responded with a laugh.

Mick declared, "Don't worry about me, Michael, I know exactly where you are," in a vaguely threatening tone that surprised Michael.

"First, I need to know she's alive" Mick continued.

Michael did not respond. Suddenly, Jillian's weak voice was on the line saying, "Mick, don't do anything for these bastards..." as the phone was whisked away from her before she could say another word.

"You've heard her, now, let's get on with it," ordered Michael.

"When I get there and my US contact hears my voice on the phone with the go ahead, Fergus will have the disk at The Cross within 2 minutes –

it's already set. No delays, you have my word," Mick promised.

Michael, knowing that The Cross would be watched by the police, started to propose a new location for the US side of the swap when unexpectedly Mick cut him off, "See you in seven hours," and banged the phone down as Michael helplessly listened to the line go dead.

Michael's fist came crashing down onto the kitchen table as he thought, *this smart little bastard knows the fucking FBI will be watching The Cross and he's got us by the balls.*

Mick turned and walked briskly toward the airline agent checking boarding passes on the 6:15 a.m. Continental flight to Belfast.

"Enjoy your trip Mr. Delaney," the Continental agent said cheerfully as she checked Mick's license and boarding pass.

Mick just smiled through his newly shaped goatee and nodded. Some trip it would be.

Chapter 27

FERGUS HAD GIVEN THE AGENTS the slip after shooting the man in the alley. He had been hiding in alleys, side streets, and taxi cabs for about eight hours when he was confident enough that he was in the clear and had mustered the courage to call Ireland with the tragic update.

Just outside a subway station in Brooklyn, he entered a phone booth and made the dreaded call to Michael with the entire terrible story. He started by confirming that he had killed the Libyans, related that Mick likely was now in federal custody spilling his guts all over the place, and ended with his own near escape and the shooting of the agent at the back of the bank so as not to be caught alive.

Michael didn't tell Fergus he was wrong about Mick being in custody and spilling his guts. He preferred to let him squirm a bit…to wallow in the muck and humiliation of his failure.

Michael was incensed but eventually revealed to Fergus that the SAMS were already in Woodcrest waiting for Fergus. In fact, they were mounted on a Bayliner boat tethered to dock in Brooklyn. The missiles themselves had already been bought and paid for. The money Fergus was to deliver to the Libyans had only been the final payment for the launch codes and exact itineraries. The launch code system had been added to the SAMs for the purpose of driving up the price, but most of the payment was for the itineraries – this information was invaluable to The New Republican Brotherhood in carrying out the attack. The missiles had arrived and been anchored to the boat a week earlier by the Libyans as part of the deal. Michael had delegated the task of receiving the boat to another member of his team on the ground in the US. It was his nature to keep even his own people in the dark about parts of the any mission as a safety measure should someone be caught. This way no one person would know everything that was planned.

Fergus listened intently, confused as to why Michael was not brow beating him or threatening his life for failure to get the launch codes and Itinerary the Libyans had stored at the bank. He breathed a sigh of relief as Michael finally explained that Mick had escaped as well and was proposing a face to face trade – the disk in exchange for Jillian.

Rejuvenated by this new information and a chance to make things right with Michael, Fergus said what he was sure Michael was already thinking, "Just make sure that wee bastard and his bitch don't live one second longer than it takes for us to get what we need."

Chapter 28

MICK SAT IN HIS SEAT staring out the window, oblivious to the clouds that floated by about an hour after takeoff as he visualized the plans he had put in motion the afternoon before. Before checking into the motel, Mick had been busy in Manhattan.

He had visited the courier service used by all of New York's top law firms – at least that was what their full-page advertisement in the Yellow Pages said. He paid the courier enough money to prioritize his assignment and to be on stand-by for Mick once he landed in Ireland. The service already had its instructions regarding two simultaneous deliveries. Mick paid the courier double the premium amount to absolutely guarantee full attention and service on what he described to the manager as a confidential and sensitive matter. Mick was placing a lot of trust in them.

More so, Mick was placing a great deal of trust in Special Agent Cecil Maxwell. *If this guy isn't great at his job, things could go horribly wrong here*, he thought.

It was dark as Mick marched through the airport after having breezed through Customs in Belfast's Aldergrove Airport. As he walked through the concourse Mick noticed that the televisions positioned at the seating areas for each gate all depicted some sort of catastrophe. Mick stopped his march toward the rental car counter and moved closer to one of the TVs. Pictures of a burned out bar and a fire that destroyed it covered the screens. Then the pictures changed to flames shooting in the air, survivors covered in soot, and medical personnel carrying out the injured and the dead. Somehow Mick could smell the fire just like he did on the day Sarah was killed. He felt his blood pressure begin to rise as the evening news anchor described the bombing of a local pub in the town of Omagh, in County Tyrone. Mick shuddered in disbelief as he heard the reporter on site say, "The New Republican Brotherhood has claimed responsibility for the bombing and continues to renounce the peace talks." All Mick could see in his mind was the image of the bomb maker with the stump for an arm sitting across from him at the breakfast table.

The news anchor went onto the next story and Mick headed for one of the Duty Free Shops where he sullenly picked up a newspaper. Mick read the headline in disgust:

OMAGH BOMBING KILLS 29
6 CHILDREN AMONG THE DEAD

He read further that the bombing threatened to disrupt the signing of the peace treaty which was being referred to in some quarters as The Good Friday Agreement, amidst speculation that it would be signed just before Easter, on Friday April 10, 1998. A major move toward peace was just three days away but Mick knew that Michael wasn't about to just let that happen.

Mick dropped the paper on the counter and resumed his march through the concourse. His eyes bulged with anger and tears as he ruminated on the fact that Michael's entire plot was just the sick bastard's way of becoming a Republican hero. Whatever it took, Mick wasn't about to let Michael kill again. He would be stopped – no matter what.

Chapter 29

FERGUS WATCHED WITH BINOCULARS from a block away as four Federal agents cased The Cross – two out front and two up the alley by the back door. Wisely, McKenna had picked The Cross as the place for Fergus to receive the disk. He knew the Feds would be there and that Fergus would have no other option but to accept the package there and then try to escape with it. McKenna had the upper hand, indeed. The New Republican Brotherhood had no other choice but to play it his way.

Michael had made clear to Fergus that doing this was his only way back into the good graces. If it meant that Fergus had to kill a couple more agents in order to get out of The Cross with the disk, Fergus was happy to do it. It was a minor complication.

Fergus kept an arsenal of guns and ammunition inside the bar behind a false wall in the basement, just in case a day like this should ever come. They were safer there than at his apartment, which he knew the Feds had searched on more than one occasion.

Getting in wasn't going to be a problem. He had already climbed the fire escape to get onto the roof at the end of the block and would easily be able to crawl slowly over all of the flat tar roofs and jump in through the skylight into the apartment that sat atop The Cross at the other end of the block of tiny row homes. Getting out would be harder. The skylight was almost twenty feet from the floor.

Although it was dangerous, he could drop down into the bathroom in the apartment, but he had no way back up. There were no ladders in the place and no chairs that would come anywhere close. He'd have to shoot his way out when the time came. At least he'd have the element of surprise since the Feds had no idea he was in there in the first place. They just sat outside waiting for him to show up – they never expected him to come from within, armed to the teeth.

Chapter 30

In the dark of night, Mick followed the reverse directions he had memorized on his way from the farmhouse with Dermot to the airport in Belfast. He'd missed many turns in his rental car due to the darkness and lack of street signs but was surprised that he didn't get turned about more than he did. Noting the time between turns had been vital, as he expected.

About a half a mile from the property, Mick ditched the car and cut across a barley field. If he had to escape with Jillian, he wanted to disappear into the night without giving his pursuers any idea what kind of car he had, or what direction he was headed. His breath grew heavy and he could see it float in the air before him as he got closer and closer to the fuzzy yellow light shining bigger and brighter from the living room where he knew Michael and Dermot sat waiting. Mick checked his watch then started up the path.

Letting out a deep breath, Mick rapped his knuckle twice on the flaking paint of the farmhouse door and turned the handle slowly. He pushed the door open and the light cut at his eyes.

Michael sat on the ragged sofa with his legs crossed, while Dermot trained an Armalite rifle on Mick's forehead as he stepped into the room. Ruairi stood in the hallway with his assault weapon down at his side. Jillian was on a folding chair with her hands tied behind her back.

"Well, the Prodigal Son returns," said Michael sarcastically.

Mick moved to the center of the room, armed with only a stare of hatred, which he directed straight into Michael's eyes.

Dermot pulled Jillian up by the hair and flung her to the ground at Mick's feet. He bent down and assured her that everything would be all right.

"Make the fucking call," commanded Michael as Dermot stepped behind Mick, searched him for weapons, then used the point of his rifle to nudge Mick over towards the table where the phone sat.

"What you want is already at The Cross. Delivered at exactly 2:00 p.m.," Mick said cockily as he looked at his watch, "...about 30 seconds ago as I walked in that door. Just have your man go to the back door."

The delivery to the feds was taking place at the same time – there was no use holding back on that now. He and

Jillian would either be killed, or they would be let go as promised. Whether they left the farmhouse dead or alive, Mick had to make sure that the feds had enough time to stop Fergus once he had the information on the disk, regardless of what happed to him and Jillian.

"Check with Fergus. It's there," Mick reiterated nervously.

Michael picked up the phone and dialed an overseas operator. Mick laughed inside at how uncomfortable Michael seemed as he fumbled through asking the operator to reverse the charges so that he could make a collect call to the United States.

Back in the US, the bartender at The Cross went to the back door as instructed by Michael and found what looked like a FedEx package lying on the ground. He took a quick glance around and saw a bike courier riding away at the end of the alley, as specifically instructed by Mick. The bartender did not immediately see agents, but he knew they had to be there. He quickly ducked back inside the bar and gave the package to Fergus, who tore apart the envelope. Inside, Fergus found the etched disk.

Fergus went into the kitchen in the back of the bar where there was a small personal computer that the owner used to cook his books. One of Fergus's crew members, who had been summoned to The Cross as soon as Fergus was safe inside, typed in the passcode from the card Fergus gave him. The disk opened up just as it had for Mick. It took about ten minutes for the man to go through the contents and he nodded to indicate that everything was there and began to print out all of the pages, most importantly the launch codes. Fergus relayed the good news to Michael.

Michael told Fergus, "You know what to do," dropped the phone into its cradle, and nodded to Dermot, seemingly to let him know that everything was there.

"OK. You have whatever it was you needed, right? So, we're leaving," Mick said as he kept one eye on Michael and slowly walked toward Jillian, bending down to help her up from the floor.

"Kill them both," Michael said calmly, his icy eyes pointed at Mick.

Dermot and Ruairi raised their weapons as ordered.

Chapter 31

MAXWELL AND HIS AGENTS had been waiting all morning and afternoon. The search for Fergus Magee was underway and after this was over some heads would roll for losing him, but for now, the FBI needed every available body to blanket the city.

Maxwell paced up and down the war room floor. Stopping, he stared out over the city and looked at his watch – 1:55 p.m. *McKenna should have called by now*, he thought.

As he started to pace again, he picked up the phone line just to make sure there was still a dial tone, wondering what danger awaited the city and why McKenna wouldn't or couldn't tell him the day before what needed to be done. McKenna had said, "You don't know the half of it." There had to be another whole side to this. McKenna was unpredictable but Maxwell was almost sure he had to be on the right side of it all. Maxwell's career depended on it and he knew it. Hell, hundreds of lives likely depended on it.

The last several weeks were a complete disaster. Finally, there had been some action in his unit, but when the bright lights were on, he and his agents had failed. From allowing their only lead Johnny Herndon to be killed on the docks in Belfast, to Fergus killing an agent then disappearing under hail of cash right in their own back yard – The Unit had failed miserably. But that wasn't even the worst of it. He was sure the SAMs would kill countless others by the end of the day unless he could stop it. Whatever this plot was, it involved the SAMs – Maxwell just needed to know when and where and his entire tactical team was ready to pounce.

Suddenly, the door of the war room flew open and in ran a receptionist in high heels.

"This was just dropped off by a bike messenger for you," she said, knowing that Maxwell had instructed the entire facility to find him as soon as any contact was made by anyone looking for him.

He cut open the Tyvek envelope. Inside was an unencrypted copy of the disk and the printouts Mick had made for him to speed up the process. Attached to the papers was the unsigned handwritten note Mick had scrawled earlier, summarizing all the documents attached and the New

Republican Brotherhood's plan. The note began with, "I know you know about the SAMs, but the lives of Prince Charles, the British ambassador, and countless civilians are at stake. You've got about six hours to find Fergus Magee. Read this all NOW."

Chapter 32

DERMOT RAISED HIS RIFLE and trained it on Mick's face. Ruairi raised his rifle as well and pointed it at Jillian, just as ordered. There was a look on Ruiari's face that told Michael something was not right. Michael's eyebrows raised in amazement as he watched Ruairi slowly spin to his left and take dead aim at Dermot.

"No. No more! No fucking more!" Ruairi said, staring directly down the sights of his gun at his compatriot.

Dermot quickly pointed his weapon straight back at Ruairi, then back at Mick, who, although unarmed, was still a threat to rush. Dermot looked over to Michael who was still on the couch for help.

"Ruairi, what the fuck are you doing? Shoot her now!" commanded Michael.

"You said Omagh was a mistake – that nobody was to die in the blast! You told me there would be more than enough time. Everyone would get out. Every last person. You lied! I made that fucking bomb and you promised me no one would die! You used it to kill kids, you fucking bastard!" he shouted.

Michael, unarmed, sat still. His loaded hand gun was steps away on the bookshelf. With Dermot and Ruairi armed, he hadn't thought he would need it when Mick arrived. He had no inkling that Ruairi would turn on his fellow men. It wasn't until now that

Ruairi had expressed any remorse over the Omagh bomb, which the New Republican Brotherhood had planted the day before.

"Ruairi, come on now. Stop being ridiculous. This is a fucking war! What happened yesterday was for all of us. For all of Ireland. You know that. What about your father? What about your brother? You know what they did to your family. Our fight must go on," Michael said, as he slowly rose from the couch.

Mick sat still as Dermot pointed his gun back and forth between Mick and Ruairi.

"Don't you fucking talk about my family! *This* is murder. *Omagh* was murder. You knew all along there'd be no real warning – didn't you? Didn't you!" he yelled at Michael.

"Surely, you are not that naïve?" Michael asked, looking down and shaking his head.

"I guess I am," Ruairi said, seemingly exhausted and beginning to weaken physically and emotionally, his hands shaking under the weight of the rifle.

"Michael, I can't do this anymore. I can't be part of this," Ruairi said, his voice trembling and his eyes welling with water as he began to lower the weapon.

Michael, sensing the opportunity, carefully inched closer to the bookshelf and said, "It's okay. That's it. Just relax. Let's talk this through."

Ruairi brought his rifle down to a level where it was mostly pointed at the floor and Dermot was able to turn his aim back towards Mick for a second.

Michael kept one eye trained on Ruairi as he felt around on the bookshelf and calmly gripped the handle of his gun.

As Michael reached for the gun and Dermot focused on Mick for a split second, Ruairi swiftly whipped his rifle upward again and squeezed the trigger.

The blast from Ruairi's rifle echoed loudly off the hard plaster walls of the farmhouse as the bullet entered the front of Dermot's forehead and blew out the back of his skull.

Michael pulled the hand gun from the shelf and swung his arm around toward Ruairi.

Mick's sneaky right hook tagged Michael squarely on the jaw just as Michael squeezed off a shot that barely missed its mark. The punch left Michael sprawled across the floor.

As Michael woozily scrambled to get up onto all fours, Mick picked up Michael's gun, stood over him and kicked him in the ribs with all of his might. Michael hit the floor again. Then, Mick, almost in a rage, pulled Michael up by his hair – right up onto his knees.

He got right into Michael's ear and spit flew out of his mouth as he angrily yelled into his face, "By the way you son of a bitch, the FBI has your precious missiles and your buddy Fergus – your plan has failed, Michael – it's a fucking disaster! It's over. We've got them both." Then, in a last surge of energy, Mick smashed Michael's head onto the hard floor one more time, knocking him out cold.

Mick looked over at Jillian as he stood there breathing heavily over the bodies of Dermot and Michael with a gun in his hand. Then, he and Jillian, both stunned by Ruairi's life saving act of courage, turned to their former captor, not knowing where this would go next.

Ruairi looked back at them with a cold blank stare then slowly walked to the table, dropped his rifle, slumped down onto a chair, and held his head in his hands as he sobbed and sobbed, muttering, "What have I done?" over and over again.

Within seconds, the farmhouse door flung open and six British Secret Service agents stormed the room, armed with rifles and bulletproof vests. Mick had no idea what was going on. He dropped the weapon and raised his hands in the air as suddenly he, Jillian, and Ruairi were all pushed down to the floor by three agents and guarded while the others searched the grounds.

The British agents had been watching the farmhouse since earlier that morning since Dermot, who was on their Most Wanted List, had been spotted in a nearby town and followed back to the hideout. Their plan had been to watch the house and gather as much intelligence on the splinter group as they could. They decided to storm the place after watching Mick walk up the path and hearing the gun shots.

The agents soon realized Jillian was a hostage and untied her. She explained Mick's involvement and finally, once convinced, and after searching Mick, they let him up. Ruairi was quickly cuffed and taken out to the barn for interrogation by the agent who had pinned him to the floor.

Mick leaned up against the wall as one of the agents knelt down to feel for a pulse on Dermot's neck. It was clear from the pool of blood and the hole in his forehead that he was dead, but protocol required confirmation.

Another agent was on his knees next to Michael trying to cuff the unconscious man at the wrists. Michael's left arm was stuck under his body. As the agent tried to roll him over to get at the trapped wrist, Michael spun swiftly, elbowed the agent in the face, grabbed hold of the gun on the agent's hip and tried to yank it from the holster. The agent grabbed hold of the holster too and struggled to keep Michael from freeing the pistol.

As the battle went on to pull the agent's gun from the holster, Mick bolted for the table where Ruairi's weapon still sat.

Mick aimed the rifle at the wrestling men but didn't have a clear shot at Michael as the two twirled and twisted round and round, each desperate for the weapon. Mick took aim over and over, each time unable to pull the trigger. Jillian ran to the back of the farmhouse to get the other agents from the barn.

Mick stood at the ready as he watched Michael bring his knee up into the groin of the agent, forcing the man to release his grip on the gun as he fell weakly to the ground.

As the agent writhed on the floor in pain, Michael stepped back, exhausted from the struggle, holding the gun at his side as he tried to catch his breath. He looked up ready to shoot Mick and anyone else between him and the door.

Initially, Michael stood in shock as he saw Mick was already pointing a rifle straight at his chest. Then, it appeared that a sense of peace came over Michael and a smile grew across his face as he realized that Mick had the draw on him and that he now stood upon the precipice of a glorious death.

"Put down the gun," Mick demanded.

"Never." responded Michael.

Then, as if in slow motion, Michael raised his gun and Mick riddled Michael's torso with gun fire, shooting until the full magazine was empty, not out of fear and not out of hatred, but to ensure that this evil man would never breathe another breath or teach another evil idea ever again.

Chapter 33

MAXWELL HUNG UP THE PHONE and ran down the stairwell to his Crown Victoria waiting in the garage. After six or seven high security calls between the bureau and the military, he was able to learn that a U.S. Army AH-64 Apache Helicopter was stationed at La Guardia Airport near Newark, New Jersey. The Apache was a helicopter that could destroy SAM sites with its Hellfire rockets. On Maxwell's way to the airport he briefed the Apache's pilot and his gunner via radio regarding the SAMs and what to prepare. There was a huge problem though. The SAM site could be anywhere. If the missiles where mounted onto a boat, it was pretty clear from the documents that there were only a few optimal points on the East River from which the missiles could be launched with clear shots at each target. However, if Fergus chose a ground launch, it could come from anywhere.

Maxwell's conference with military personnel confirmed that the launch code pads on the SAMS depicted in the schematics where a modification added to what were normally weapons deployed by trigger alone. The consensus was that this security feature had been added by the Libyans as a safety measure, and possibly so that they could extract more money from the IRA after physical delivery. The paperwork also appeared to depict customization by the Libyans that provided for both heat seeking hand launch and the programming of preset coordinates to strike stationary targets and the coordinates provided within the documents lead directly to the UN. Most importantly, Maxwell learned that the missiles only had about a 2.9 mile range, which narrowed the potential launch area, however, if Fergus was going to use a truck, he could launch from just about any open area near the river on Manhattan, or in Brooklyn or Queens. There was no way they could cover every access point on the river and there was no way to blanket the shore lines of all three places at once.

Since the Apache was an attack helicopter, it was manufactured to hold a two man crew – the gunner and the pilot. An emergency seat in a tiny cargo area was all that remained. Maxwell climbed up and strapped into the small seat tucked behind the pilot in the cargo space. As he pulled on his helmet and headset, the pilot turned and gave him the thumbs up as the Apache began to lift off.

Maxwell took a deep breath and blew it out slowly. He knew when the attack would be thanks to Mick. However, Fergus was still in the wind and the attack could come from anywhere. While Maxwell prepared for a worst case scenario air attack, Jensen's team and the entire FBI in New York and North Jersey was searching for Fergus on the ground. Fergus didn't know that the feds already knew when he would launch the missiles and had already cleared the target areas; however, there were hundreds of entry points on the NY and NJ side for a boat docked on the river and a million open spaces on land from which to launch from a truck. They simply couldn't cover them all, even with the help of the NYPD. The real goal was to make sure Fergus never got to the missiles in the first place. But where the hell was he?

As the agents sat across from the bar, all seemed quiet. The front door to The Cross was locked and no one was coming or going. Fergus hadn't been seen since he was throwing cash all over Manhattan but The Cross had to be watched nonetheless. Little did they know, he had crept in through the skylight hours earlier.

Fergus knew getting out would be tough. But he had the weaponry to do it. He stepped through the back door of the kitchen into the garage behind the bar where an old Ford F150 pickup awaited. He turned on the ignition and was careful not to rev the motor, lest he lose the element of surprise.

The white splintered wood of the garage door flew everywhere as the truck ploughed through the closed garage door with Fergus hanging out the window shooting a machine gun while he spun around the corner and headed for the ramp to I-287.

The two FBI cars that had been watching The Cross where caught off-guard by Fergus driving through a closed garage door and barely were able to return fire as they ducked in their seats before beginning pursuit of the red truck.

As they chased Fergus through residential areas at speeds that reached 60 miles per hour, the agents radioed Jensen over by the UN, describing the pickup truck and the fact that it had a covered bed, which they believed housed the mounted missiles. Jensen radioed Maxwell to tell him that apparently the attack would be made from the ground but couldn't reach him. Jenson knew Maxwell was likely already at the airport where his walkie might be intermittently jammed by air traffic control. Regardless, Jensen got the message out to everyone else available and all FBI and NYPD resources where now focused on stopping a ground launch.

Up on the highway, Fergus weaved in and out of traffic that was surprisingly light for a work day. He could see the feds chasing behind, about ten cars back. The traffic was heavy enough that the agents could not shoot at him but light enough that he could use the ability to change lanes suddenly to his advantage.

He approached eighty miles per hour as he flew over the Triborough Bridge and drove through the toll booth lane almost as fast. He had to drive on parts of the sidewalk down 31st Street due to a traffic jam. Two NYPD cars joined the chase as he headed over the Pulaski Bridge.

Driving with reckless abandon was fun. Fergus thought about OJ Simpson, who led the police on a high speed chase four years earlier. His chase was much slower and a lot less exciting – plus he got caught. There was no way Fergus would be caught. Not alive at least.

He had enough of a lead on the cops now that he knew they would not catch him before he made it to the East River. At a dock near Gee Avenue in Brooklyn, down by Wallabout Channel, just north of the Brooklyn Navy Yard, Fergus jumped from the truck and the yellow Bayliner speedboat sat dockside, right where Michael said it would be. White tarp was stretched across part of its bay, covering its military cargo.

Fergus jumped down into the boat with his automatic rifle and felt around under the rear seat cushion for the keys that had been hidden there just for him.

The dual Mercury motors fired up strong as the police and FBI cars drove up to the dock. Fergus pulled the throttle back and the tip of the craft rose up from the water and beautiful white wakes of foam shot out from each side of the speed boat.

Fergus was about 100 yards from shore when the 7 or 8 cops on the dock began shooting. A few shots hit the side of Bayliner's hull but nothing that would make her sink. The salty river water sprayed up into Fergus's eyes as the wind whipped his long gray hair all around his face. He stood with one hand on the wheel, scratched at his scraggly beard and then waved goodbye, flashing a sinister smile as the agents stood there helplessly. The name on the back of the boat mocked the two FBI agents who read it. The NYPD cops on the dock had no idea what the Gaelic phrase "Tiochfaidh ar la" meant and probably never even noticed it on the back of the boat. But all of the agents in the Western Europe Counter Terrorism Division knew the IRA rallying cry all too well. It meant merely, "Our time will come."

At least it was finally clear – the attack would come from the river.

Atop the city skyline in the apache helicopter Maxwell confirmed with ground forces at the United Nations via satellite phone that the Summit had been adjourned for security reasons and that Prince Charles was now sitting in an FBI safe house nowhere near downtown Manhattan. The building itself and the five blocks surrounding it were evacuated due to a "bomb scare." *What an understatement,* he thought. The transport helicopter carrying the Ambassador had been secretly rerouted to McGuire Air Force Base in New Jersey, from where he would head back to England. The targets that Fergus had in mind would not be where he expected them to be, but there was no way for Fergus to know that. It likely wouldn't have mattered any way. Fergus was on the run and Maxwell was relatively sure that the missiles would be launched in any scenario.

Maxwell's satellite phone rang as the sun approached the horizon.

"Maxwell, come in," he yelled into the microphone as the whooping thud of the helicopters blades filled the aircraft.

"Fergus is in the river, over," responded Jensen.

"Dammit!" yelled Maxwell, "Where? Over."

"He slipped in from a small dock in Brooklyn. He's on a speed boat. NYPD boats are headed straight for him but they were patrolling the north end of the river when he went in. He's coming from the south and will be within launch range before they can get to him. Over," Jensen reported.

Maxwell checked the timing with the pilot. "We're three minutes out, over" said Maxwell, knowing that the only way to stop Fergus now was from the air.

"Good luck, boss. Over," said Jensen.

"We'll need it. Over," said Maxwell turning to the pilot and the gunner.

"Take the flight path that the Ambassador was to take," Maxwell directed through his headset microphone. The pilot, looking straightforward, acknowledged with a thumbs up.

As the Apache banked left, cutting through the air like an arrow, the sun started to dip down behind the brilliant New York City skyline and a thousand colors exploded through the sky.

Chapter 34

FERGUS CHECKED HIS MAP and cut the motors along with the boat's running lights. He was within range. He still had a few minutes before the Ambassador's helicopter was scheduled to cross the river. He unlatched the cord that strapped down the vinyl covering that was stretched over the SAMs. The large SAM was mounted to the deck of the boat with large bolts and would be used for the UN. Fergus dialed in the UN coordinates on the large missile. The smaller SAM was to be shot from his shoulder as the Ambassador flew overhead. It was heat seeking and would blow the helicopter right from the air with ease.

Fergus positioned the Bayliner so that its tip faced the darkening silhouette of the UN Building about a mile ahead on his left, then dropped the anchor. The current of the river kept the boat fairly straight. When the time was right, all he needed to do was enter the activation code, push a green button to start the hydraulics that raised the missile to an angle high enough to clear the front of the watercraft, then hit LAUNCH. But, first, he'd take care of the Ambassador.

There was some traffic on the river but Fergus went unnoticed by the occasional commercial vessel and recreational cruiser. Most of the river had been cleared by the feds but anyone that had previously been out on the bay was still headed to the docks that lined the shores of Manhattan, Queens, and Brooklyn. None of the boats came close enough to see anything Fergus had on board. He sat silently waiting as the river darkened and then he heard the blades of the helicopter.

"Right on time he whispered," as he pressed the access code on the keypad and raised the missile up onto his shoulder.

Maxwell had received an update from Jensen describing the Bayliner and its yellow hull. Still, in the graying hue of the evening, with several small watercraft in the same location where he expected Fergus to be, the Bayliner was hard for the pilot and the gunner to spot.

Fergus held the SAM tight and focused in through the sights. The whirly bird was crossing the river at a slow pace which was easy to track.

His heart began to thump with expectation.

The click of the trigger in his hand was exhilarating. Then suddenly, Fergus was catapulted back onto the floor a millisecond after he released his finger and lost his footing on the wet decking of the boat as the missile fired up and shot out of the housing that remained in his hand. As he gathered himself hurriedly and rolled up onto his knees so he wouldn't miss the spectacle, he watched as the trail of smoke and flame lit up the sky behind his beautiful projectile. "Fuck you, Sir Christopher Meyer," he whispered.

The gunner was the first to see the bright light and simultaneously a radar alarm went off inside the Apache to signal the approaching weapon.

The gunner coolly stated, "In coming. Portside Hellfire activated."

Maxwell braced himself by grabbing at the sides of his seat.

Fergus stood with his hands white-knuckled on the steering wheel in anticipation of the glorious destruction of the helicopter which carried one of his motherland's enemies.

The Apache pilot deftly stopped the aircraft on a dime and gyrated it to face the SAM. The gunner locked in on the approaching missile, shifted the stick in front of him, and the entire Apache wiggled ever so slightly up, down, and then side to side, hovering as the kid from Ohio scanned his dials and took aim.

"Target acquired. Firing," said the gunner, calm, in the comfort of routine, as off-handedly as a man ordering a tuna sandwich.

Fergus squinted and scrunched up his nose trying to figure out why the helicopter had stopped and turned toward the SAM. A half a second later, he was bewildered by the sight of the entire night's sky lighting up and the massive explosion that followed as a rocket from the helicopter and the SAM hit head-on over the water, causing a blast as loud and as spectacular as a hundred fireworks grand finales.

Fergus stood stunned for a split second then snapped out of it. This was not the British Ambassador. He had to move, now. He hit a button and the anchor began to pull up from the river's floor. He did not wait for the anchor to make it all the way back up to the boat before he pulled the throttle full speed ahead. He needed to move fast.

Maxwell needlessly reminded the pilot and gunner that there was still another missile on board the boat and the Apache swooped down and headed straight toward the Bayliner.

Fergus raced to catch up with a huge private yacht that appeared to be headed for the 34th Street dock. He knew if he could get close enough the Apache would need to disengage or otherwise risk collateral damage in the form of civilians lives lost to another Hellfire rocket.

Maxwell's sight lines were not great from the back seat but he knew the Apache was right on Fergus.

"Take the shot," he pleaded.

"Sorry, Sir. He's too close to another boat. The blast area is too great. All we can do is trail him now," the gunner replied.

As Fergus struggled to stay close to the yacht in light of the much larger ship's huge wake, he saw the halogen lights of an NYPD river patrol boat charging toward him from up river. The police boat swung wide and circled in behind him about fifty yards back.

The yacht's wake proved to be too much for the small Bayliner and eventually Fergus lost control for a split second and slipped away from the much larger boat, giving the NYPD its chance to attack.

This was a "shoot on sight" situation and each of the four officers on the boat had been given that directive. The NYPD officers converged on Fergus, shooting at every part of the boat they could hit. Fergus was not top side.

Suddenly, Fergus popped up from the cabin hole on the top of the boat's bow and began wildly shooting an AK-47 at the police, as the officers took their own cover within the small river boat.

As soon as the officers took cover, Fergus went down into the cabin then crept on all fours to the captain's wheel once again. As he accelerated full speed toward the NYPD boat, he knelt down and steered with the bottom of the steering wheel so as to be protected by the hull while he rammed his foe's vessel. The NYPD boat was in the Bayliner's path now and the captain was not able to move quickly enough to avoid being rammed. The bow of Fergus's boat tore through the center of the NYPD boat, capsizing it while the Bayliner soared into the air and bounced twice, eventually landing flat on the river.

Fergus was thrown to the back of the boat and the side of his face gushed with blood from having been struck and ripped open by the sharp mounting hardware that held the remaining missile. He crawled to the helm of the boat and tried to turn the outboard motors on but nothing happened. Looking back towards the rear of the Bayliner he saw that one of the motors was completely gone and that the police boat was upside down with officers scrambling for shore in their life jackets. To his rear he saw the lights of two more NYPD boats approaching from the south. Fergus ran back and pulled the choke then tried the ignition key again. A terrible sound came from the back of the boat as the motor was grinding and smoking, but he was moving. He got about 500 yards away before the second motor died too.

Maxwell watched on as the pilot called the NYPD and passed on Maxwell's request that each NYPD boat focus on the rescue effort. The pursuit of Fergus from the water needed to stop to clear the way for the Hellfire rocket. It was time to end this thing.

Fergus rushed to the SAM. He pulled the code numbers from his pocket and entered them quickly as the blood from his head poured down his face and hair, all over the key pad. The back of the boat was now filling with water and the *Tiochfaidh ar la* was about to sink. The Apache's blades were thumping overhead. Fergus quickly pushed the green button and the hydraulic started to raise the missile.

The second Hellfire rocket had been locked and loaded on Fergus since he had launched the first SAM. Now he was far enough away from the yacht and police boats for the gunner to take a clear shot.

The hydraulics slowly cranked upward. Fergus impatiently stole a quick glance at the helicopter. The tip of the SAM began to crest the bow of the boat and Fergus stood defiantly one last time, shaking his fist at the sky as the warhead on the Hellfire rocket struck dead center of the Bayliner blowing Fergus, his SAM, and his entire world into a sea of blazing smithereens.

Chapter 35

MICK AND JILLIAN had been questioned at the tiny local police station for sixteen hours before they received word that they were free to leave. FBI personnel from London and high-ranking officials in the British Secret Service had grilled them both about every detail. About eight hours in, the FBI agents confirmed for Mick that Fergus had been stopped and killed, then handed him a wired communication that simply read:

Mick,

Thanks. When you get back to the US maybe we can grab a cup of coffee.

Regards
Cecil Maxwell,
Special Agent-in-Charge,
Federal Bureau of Investigation

Even after handing over the thank you note from the man in charge back in the US, the FBI agents who were stationed in the UK didn't miss the chance to berate Mick for leaving the FBI in the dark simply to save Jillian. Their tongue lashing was a small price to pay for Jillian's life in Mick's opinion.

As Mick walked out of his interrogation room, Jillian was being led out of hers. Mick took her in his arms and she broke down crying. He held her tight as tears soaked the front of his shirt. A police officer entered the hallway and offered them a ride wherever they needed to go. Jillian said she just wanted to be taken home and looked on silently as Mick declined the offer.

"Where will you go?" she asked.

"I'm not sure. I need to be alone right now," he offered.

"I understand," said Jillian as she wiped her eyes and stared down at the floor. She thought about the fact that Mick still hadn't completely dealt with the loss of Sarah and needed time to work things out in his mind. Then, she brought her hand up to the side of Mick's face, cupped it gently and kissed him on the lips, and said, "Thank you, Mick. I will never forget you."

Mick leaned back, cracked a wry smile and said, "I wouldn't think so."

Jillian laughed through tears as Mick let her hand slip from his and started up the hallway.

Mick headed out the police station door into the bright sunlight and took a left down a dirt road, walking with no destination in mind. He'd find a bus somewhere at some point and make his way back to Shannon Airport and eventually the US. But for now, he was content to just walk and think.

It took a few hours on the twisting country roads for him to review the last two days in his mind, and several more hours for his mind to finally relax and his anxiety to *begin* to release a bit.

Down every road he turned, the countryside shone beautifully under the dazzling sun. It reminded him of Sarah, how beautiful she was and how sadly her life had ended. Tears strolled down his face as he marveled at the beautiful yet troubled land stretched out before him. He was confused and damaged and had no idea where his life would go next. But he knew that the peace and freedom he had back in the US before Sarah was killed was something he would never look at the same way again.

For three days Mick wandered wherever the road led him. He rested on a bench the first night in a little village somewhere, crossed the border the following day, and thumbed his way to the West coast the next. He headed south along the coast line, walking and hitching rides, then ended up in the small fishing village of Dingle. Inside the warmth of a cozy fish and chip shop, sitting before a scorching hot cup of tea and a fry, Mick scanned the front page of *The Irish Times.* The banner at the top of the page pointed the readership to stories about Van Morrison's East Belfast roots and a report from Augusta National back in the States where The Masters golf tournament was underway in Georgia. The major headline underneath read, "HISTORIC AGREEMENT MARKS A NEW BEGINNING FOR US ALL."

The article went on to tell the story of the signing of the Good Friday Agreement, which would be ratified a month later by an overwhelming majority in both the North and the South. Northern Ireland would be given its freedom and complete home rule would be established. The North would also have the right to stay part of Britain if it so chose. Eight hundred years of English domination was over and no longer would the rivers in Ireland be all that ran free.

Mick sipped his tea and closed his eyes. He was tired. It was time to head home.

EPILOGUE
SIX MONTHS LATER

Chapter 36

THE DAY'S CATCH had been sorted, unloaded and weighed. Mick's muscles were sore from pulling nets and traps for eight hours. The work was hard but he enjoyed the solitude and physical labor which came with being out on the open sea. He'd resigned from the University shortly after arriving home. He just couldn't go there anymore.

Captain Bradshaw had agreed to stay on for a while until Mick, who worked as the third mate, learned more about the workings of the small commercial boat that fished the Atlantic shores.

For months after Mick got back to Philadelphia he received daily voice messages from the attorney who had handled Sarah's will. Every message explained that Sarah's life insurance carrier had sent the check to the attorney who drafted her will since Mick, who was the beneficiary on the policy, never returned their calls in the weeks following her death. Mick wanted nothing to do with the money.

Mick wallowed in his grief and alcohol for weeks, barely getting out of bed for days at a time. The nightmares came and went as did waking up to his own screams in a cold sweat. He barely ate and empty bottles of beer and whiskey littered his once tidy apartment. His phone rang and rang as he sat and watched old reruns on TV day after day. His family desperately tried to help, coming to the apartment every couple of days to check on him and make sure he had food. He assured them he was fine. After the police found him walking the streets shirtless one night, searching for an open bar at 3 a.m., Mick realized he had finally hit bottom. At the police station, he finally agreed to get some help at the request of his father who had come to claim him.

The first few sessions were tough. Mick simply sat back and listened to the other men who had lost their wives spew their terrible stories. Six weeks in, he began to feel a sense of healing as he sat and heard these others who had lost their greatest loves put it all out there right on the table for everyone else to see. Somehow it helped to know that he was not alone. Soon, he started to feel like he was able to breathe again and eventually he began to tell his story of loss and agony. It was cathartic and freeing. His hurt had been eating him up from the inside out and sharing it all with these kindred spirits was like a confession that left him feeling warm and alive inside. He still thought about Sarah everyday but his head was filled not with morbid thoughts, rather he felt as sense of peace and joy as he remembered their great life together. He was heading toward a good place again and he felt his soul come alive once more.

As he healed, he often thought of the day he spent in Killybegs near the Morrissey's campsite, where he once sat on the bench and watched the fisherman put in their hard day's work. That day he had wondered what it would have been like to live that life.

Now, he was the owner of a fishing boat. Captain Bradshaw was retiring and Sarah's life insurance was more than enough to cover the cost. The Captain sold the boat and the fishing business to Mick on the stipulation that he would keep all of the crew as part of the deal. Mick wouldn't have had it any other way. Eventually, Bradshaw would leave and the First Mate would take the helm until Mick worked his way up. It humbled Mick but gave him something to look forward to each day – a challenge and a goal that got him out of bed each and every morning.

Each night, as the *Sarah-Mairead* returned from the sea and headed towards the docks, Mick stared out at the setting October sun and thought about the two women after whom he had named the boat. He'd written to Big Tom who cried on the phone when he called to thank Mick, not only for naming the boat after his daughter, but also for all that he had done and all that he had risked in order to save Jillian.

As Mick jumped down onto the dock and tied off the last mooring line, he waived to Bradshaw who was still up in the wheelhouse of the ship. It wouldn't be long until the Captain was gone and Mick was in no rush to see him go. Life was good now and Mick needed as much time as possible to learn the business. There was no rush.

With a spring in his step, Mick jogged down the dock and across the crushed stone parking lot to his car, approached it from the rear, walked down its left side, and opened the door to jump in. Then he caught himself. He made the mistake every so often and it made him laugh each time. A few times he had even opened the door fully and sat down in the seat on the left side of the car expecting to see a steering wheel in front of him, just like back home. He wondered whether he would ever fully get used to the steering wheel being on the right side of the car and driving on the left side of the road. Thankfully, he didn't have to worry about that when steering just off the shores of Killybegs each day when Captain Bradshaw gave him his lessons on how to steer the ship. There were no lanes out on the ocean just off the shore of west Ireland.

As he sat in the car and headed towards Morrissey's Campsite to see Jillian again for the first time, he wondered how she would react to his having moved to Ireland. He planned to ask her to take a ride up North to have a drink at Finlay's, the bar where they had connected the first night. While he thought of where a life with Jillian might lead, he couldn't help but think of Sarah. He'd come to realize there was no one person responsible for her death – that her death was simply a byproduct of evil and hatred.

The evil and hatred that killed Sarah was that which lived in Dermot and Michael and that which lived inside the person who set the bomb that took her life that fatal day. Despite the thought, he smiled to himself as he basked in the realization that, through it all, he had learned the true meaning of life. To love with all of your heart and to never let that love go. Maybe that was why the people of Ireland had so much trouble being at peace – their unwavering love of this great country. At least, now, after 800 years, Ireland was finally at some sort of peace. There would always be some evil people on both sides that would threaten to disturb the peace in Ireland – but Mick now knew that he would never leave her again. He had been inexplicably drawn back across the sea and wondered whether it had to do with the Irish blood that coursed through his veins. As the rays from the setting sun behind him reflected off the rearview mirror into Mick's face, it struck him for the first time that this troubled country and this troubled man were now one – and that, finally, both were at peace.

He slowed the car and turned into the campsite driveway, excited to begin what he hoped would be the next chapter in what he now saw as a beautiful life.

Historical Note

For purposes of plot, the timeframe of the Omagh bombing as depicted in the historical fiction novel *Irish Blood* has been changed. In the novel, the bomb exploded just *before* the signing of The Good Friday Agreement and was planted by a fictional IRA splinter group. However, in actuality, the horrific bombing took place on August 15, 1998, four months later, *in response to* the signing of The Good Friday Agreement and was carried out by an actual IRA splinter group named the Real Irish Republican Army, killing 29 people and injuring hundreds more.

Brendan Sean Sullivan

Printed in Germany
by Amazon Distribution
GmbH, Leipzig